"I'm sorry you ▮▮▮▮▮
Cate said.

Nick said nothing. What was there to say? He had taken lives today for the first—and he hoped last—time. Right now, he was pretty revved up and the anger was still ruling. Later, he suspected the impact of what he'd done would hit him.

"You're trained to save lives," Cate said as if reading his mind. It was disconcerting. Hell, everything that had happened since she came back into his life had been disconcerting.

She had shot someone today, too, he remembered. "Did it bother you?" he asked.

"Yes, but there's no choice. Well, there was one, but when it's live or die, I'm gonna choose live every time." There were tears in her eyes

He eased out of traffic, turned down a dirt road and parked behind trees. "Come here," he said gently. She slid her arms around his waist, laid her head on his shoulder and held him tight. For several long moments, he simply held her close

Dear Reader,

What do people do when they can no longer work in their chosen profession? How do they totally reinvent themselves? I've seen this done, up close and personal, and it's no easy task, giving up that in-the-know status, that feeling of being right in the middle of life-changing events, doing everything you can to fix them. And suddenly, you're on the outside of it all.

As with any drastic upheaval in life, it helps to have a support system, but I wondered what would happen if that was also taken away. Here is the story of two individuals, dedicated to their jobs to the exclusion of all else, who are forced together by duty and circumstance. Can they help each other deal with the emotional trauma while dodging both danger and a passion they've denied for years?

Read on to see how COMPASS Special Agent Cate Olin and neurosurgeon Nick Sandro tackle their demons after the fall....

Enjoy!

Lyn Stone

The Doctor's MISSION

Lyn Stone

Silhouette®

Romantic

SUSPENSE

SILHOUETTE BOOKS

ISBN-13: 978-0-373-27604-2
ISBN-10:   0-373-27604-4

THE DOCTOR'S MISSION

Visit Silhouette Books at www.eHarlequin.com

Printed in U.S.A.

Books by Lyn Stone

LYN STONE

A painter of historical events, Lyn decided to write about them. A canvas, however detailed, limits characters to only one moment in time. "If a picture's worth a thousand words, the other ninety thousand have to show up somewhere!"

An avid reader, she admits, "At thirteen, I fell in love with Bronte's Heathcliff and became Catherine. Next year, I fell for Rhett and became Scarlett. Then I fell for the hero I'd known most of my life and finally became myself."

After living four years in Europe, Lyn and her husband, Allen, settled into a log house in north Alabama that is crammed to the rafters with antiques, artifacts and the stuff of future tales.

For my Al, master of reinvention, soul of inspiration and forever the very heart of me.

Prologue

Bernese Alps, Switzerland, November 6th

Sunlight sparkled off the perfectly powdered slope. Thin, crisp air added to the euphoria zinging through Cate Olin's veins as she looked out over the awesome peaks surrounding her. "On top of the world," she sighed.

Cate tossed her companion a smile. Werner looked almost as impressive as the scenery. Together, he and the Alps would make a terrific travel ad for winter fun and games. And she would spend no more time with him than she would with these mountains.

He had approached her in the bar last night and asked her to dance. They'd talked, laughed, danced some more and then he had suggested they ski together the next morning. So here she was, having some much-needed fun, her reward for a tough mission accomplished.

After a light breakfast at Le Chalet d'Adrien, they had caught a hop, then ridden the lift to the top of Col des Gentianes to ski off-piste. Werner said it was supposed to be a fun run. A friend of his had highly recommended it.

Werner adjusted his goggles, then his gloves. She would love to know what he was thinking right now, but telepathy did not work on this guy. That was okay, too. That skill required concentration and mental energy. Her last assignment had taken a lot out of her and she badly needed a couple of weeks of nothing but recreation.

He slid slowly to her side, their skis parallel as he leaned sideways to kiss her cheek. "Ready to rock and roll?"

His Austrian accent was cute and he knew it. Cate took a second simply to enjoy the way he looked. She toyed with the idea of sleeping with him later. She might. And she might not.

Sex without any deep emotional involvement would be a new experience for her and one she thought she might find more depressing than satisfying. She sensed Werner didn't do *deep*.

"Give me a minute." She adjusted the bright red cap she wore and determined not to worry about anything today.

Cate shook the tension out of her legs one at a time, lifting each ski as she relaxed her muscles. She shrugged her shoulders to loosen them, then set her poles and grinned at Werner. "Okay, let's boogie!"

"Take the lead." He gestured broadly for her to go ahead of him. "I would like to watch your derriere!"

Cate hesitated, then experienced one of those *uh-oh* moments when he gave her a playful shove and shouted, "Go, you little chicken!"

Laughing, she wanted to glance back, but had to gain her balance and keep it. The bright morning sun had paved the powder with a slick-as-glass surface.

Cate flew, unable to control her speed the way she wished. The slopes she had experienced before had been bumpy with the tracks of others, offering a bit of traction. And not this steep. She slalomed, attempting to brake, tried to snow plow to no avail, then considered falling down, just to stop her rapid descent.

After a harrowing run, the trail leveled out a little where it edged against a steep incline on her right. Suddenly she heard a distinctive crack, then another. *A rifle!*

Ten feet to her left, the slope dropped off like a cliff's edge. To her right, the snow covered wall. Above, the rumble of an avalanche. No accident of nature.

She dug in her poles, pushed hard and picked up speed, trying to outrun the fall, go perpendicular to it, get out of its way. To God knew what. But someone had skied this way earlier today. The trail led somewhere besides over the edge of an abyss. She hoped.

Snow pelted her head and shoulders, slid down, obliterated her path. There was nowhere to go but over the edge, where the descending rush of snow would take her anyway if it didn't cover and smother her here.

Instinctively, Cate tucked her poles beneath her arms, squatted down and fell sideways. She snapped off her skis, scrambled for the cliff's edge and looked over for a safe way down. A rolling crush of white shoved her from behind and took her with it.

As white blanked out the blue of the sky, Cate fought panic. She struggled to stay on the surface. Couldn't let it bury her. The heat from her body would encase her in ice in less than half an hour. If the oxygen trapped with her lasted that long and the weight of the snow didn't crush her.

Then she hit something really hard that broke her slide and she began to tumble head over heels.

She wanted to scream, but her mouth wouldn't move. She closed her eyes and took a deep breath, knowing it could be full of snow and the last one she would ever take.

Chapter 1

Martigny Hospital, Valais, Switzerland—November 27th

Nick Sandro swore under his breath. He knew what he had to do. His parents had put it to him like an order. *Look after Cate.* Friendship demanded it. He had no excuse not to. He had done it reluctantly during the greater parts of their childhood and adolescence. He would have to do it now.

Bracing himself, he pushed open the door of her hospital room. "Hi, Catie," he said softly. "You awake?"

Her smile looked as forced as his felt. "Hey, Nick. They told me you were here. It was good of you to come."

"Glad to," he said with a shrug. "Besides, Mom and

Dad would have my head if I didn't come and see about you."

"Like old times, huh? Trying to match us up." Tears leaked from her right eye, but the smile stayed in place.

She looked frail. Her long, straight hair had been snipped close to her scalp in the area around her incision. The rest lay lank and lifeless around her pale, striking features. She had wide, dark-lashed eyes of the deepest blue imaginable, a straight no-nonsense nose and a luscious mouth that begged kissing. Even after all this time, he could still recall the feel of those lips and the taste of her as she'd kissed him. The sensation still raised guilt. He had been twenty. She had been jailbait.

"How are they?" she asked.

"Fine," he said, keeping his voice bright. "Dad's in London at a seminar. Mom went along. They'll stay for a vacation and return home in a few weeks."

"Yeah, they sent me a card. Picture of the horse guards," Cate said with a chuckle. "Inside, it said *Giddyup*."

Nick laughed with her, losing a little of the wariness he felt. "Serious get-well wish."

"Karen? How's she?"

"Pregnant. Divorced again. She should have known better than to marry another doctor." He grimaced automatically, but added a small laugh to show he wasn't carrying a torch for his ex-wife.

Cate smiled at him. "She's a real dunce, that girl."

He nodded, smiling. "It was a mistake. We're both wiser."

She sighed heavily. Her smile remained, wistful but

sincere. Nick wondered if Cate ever regretted passing on marriage. As far as he knew she had never shown the slightest interest in it. He had kept pretty close tabs over the years through their parents. "How about this Austrian you were with on the slopes? Important?"

The smile crooked a bit. "Mostly to himself. But he did save my bacon when he called for the rescue."

"But the bastard didn't try to dig you out. I'd like to break his neck."

"Judging by the tracks, they think he *did* try after he called in. One of his skis was found near where I was buried. Apparently, he fell on the way or was caught in a secondary slide. They probably won't find him until spring thaw."

"So he wasn't involved in trying to kill you."

"Somebody probably paid him to ski that particular slope. He was pretty insistent we do that one. Jack said Werner made a cash deposit in his account the day before, but it wasn't enough to hire someone to conspire in a murder. True, Werner was a little vain, but I know he was no killer."

Nick saw a tear trickle down her cheek, but she didn't seem to be really grieving over the man, just sad that he'd been lost.

Even without makeup, hair a mess and dressed in a wrinkled, faded hospital gown, Cate was the most beautiful woman he knew. She was tall, nearly six feet; her body was angular, yet very graceful. He noted her nails were clipped to the quick with no polish, making her supple, long-fingered hands look smaller than he remembered.

The need to hold and reassure her hit him like a fist every time he looked at her. He hadn't worried enough about his own reactions before taking this on. Maybe he should have examined his reasons a little more carefully. No way could he let them seclude her in some safe house without the kind of help she would need, though, no matter how hard this got for him. The government might furnish doctors to check on her, but who was to say what sort and whether they would be concerned about anything other than her vital signs.

Cate was observing him closely. "You're looking good, Nick. Still plundering around in people's gray matter?" she asked as a brave attempt at being chipper.

He looked away from her direct blue gaze. "I'm taking some time off."

"Knocking around Florence, Jack says. Working vacation?"

"Sort of. I came over a few months ago. Attending some seminars at the Johns Hopkins campus there."

"Teaching them how to cut?" she asked, blunt as ever.

"No, not teaching." So she didn't know what had happened. Hadn't heard. What had proved a life-changing event for him hadn't even warranted a paragraph in the local paper. No one had died, after all. He hadn't really been on duty when it had happened, just in the wrong place at the wrong time. His parents would not have mentioned the incident to her except to relate how lucky he was to have escaped death.

No, he was the only one who felt the full impact of his injury. He could no longer operate. His career was over.

No reason Cate *should* have heard about it. Oddly enough, she was probably the only one who would fully understand. Eventually she would, but he couldn't dump that on her now. She had enough problems of her own.

"Odd that you'd choose Florence," she said. "I would have thought Rome. Isn't that where your grandparents were from?"

He nodded. Her parents came in just then and he turned to greet them. "See you later," he said to Cate. "I'll leave you to your visit."

Jack Mercier, Cate's boss, was waiting for Nick in the lounge across the hall. "Did you tell her?" he asked, frowning.

"Not yet," Nick said. "I'm still not sure…"

"She'll be safe with you in Florence. Safer than anywhere else she could go. I'll station eyes there in case you run into trouble."

Eyes? Agents that surveilled, no doubt. That whole business was foreign to him, the terminology as strange as medical terms would be to Cate. Yet another barrier between them. Good. He could use more of those.

Mercier headed up the elite counter-terrorist organization Cate had been working as an undercover operative for these past couple of years. Nick thought Cate had been working as an intelligence analyst at a desk somewhere in Washington. God only knew what her duties had entailed. *Had* being the key word. She was finished.

Mercier's voice dropped to a confidential tone. "I have to ask, Sandro. Are you physically capable of firing a weapon if you need to?" He glanced pointedly at Nick's right hand, permanently damaged in an E.R. confrontation with a crackhead nearly a year ago when he had stopped in on an informal consult. Mercier pressed. "You *are* left-handed, right?"

Nick flexed his fingers out of habit. "I used to shoot skeet and I could still pull a trigger, but there's no way I'm qualified to give Cate the protection you say she might need."

"I only ask as a precaution. You'll have bodyguards keeping a close watch." He ran a hand through his hair and shook his head. "Take her to Florence, help with her rehab and give me an evaluation. That's all you have to do."

"That's *all?*" Nick gave a wry huff. "Right."

"We have a good protection program, as I told you before, but I really think she'll have a better chance of recovery with the help of someone she knows. She needs that with what she'll be facing. You spoke to Dr. Ganz. You know what she's up against. Want her to do that with strangers who are just doing their jobs?"

Every instinct of self-preservation within Nick warned against it. Not because someone might still be gunning for Cate. If anything, that was the most compelling argument Mercier had for convincing Nick to agree.

He had been living in Florence the last few months, attending the seminars. After Cate's injury, the Olins had contacted his parents and asked them to plead their case. They wanted someone they knew to see that Cate was getting the best medical help available. They had obviously spoken with Mercier, who had roped him in to helping her with therapy.

"Do you have any idea who tried to kill her?" he asked. What had happened had been no accident. Mercier had stationed guards outside her door since she'd been admitted. "What about the man she was with that day?"

"He called for rescue and was pinpointing Cate's location when he was cut off midsentence. He's still missing. He said he heard the shots that caused the avalanche. When Cate regained consciousness, she verified there was gunfire, definitely a rifle. We think maybe he was going to dig her out and got buried in a drift. One way or another, we'll find him."

"Any new suspects?"

Jack nodded. "Yes. Two of our operatives coordinating with the Police Nationale have someone under surveillance now, a known assassin who was spotted in the area. It's a matter of time before they make an arrest, maybe only hours. But even if he is our shooter, somebody hired him for it. I'd like to have Cate stashed somewhere she can't be found."

"Why would someone want to kill her? And why that way?"

"We'll have some answers soon. Sam Jakes, a freelance reporter from D.C., blew her cover the week before this happened. He must have had an inside track at the White House. That was a very private ceremony with only our teams, the president and a couple of staff present. Jakes reported the commendation she received and explained her part in the investigation. Unfortunately, he gave her name, a recent photo and some background material on her."

"So she was outed and you think some wacko read that and is after her? Did you arrest the bastard who did the article?"

"Of course. The point is, that put Cate at great risk."

"So she would no longer be good for covert work anyway?"

"I'd planned to have her doing backup or mop up, not as primary. At least not for a while. Now, because of this injury, any type of field work is out of the question. Whatever she does for us, we'll have to keep her under wraps. She's made enemies. We'll get whoever is after her. In the meantime, all you need to do is keep her with you and take care of her health."

"And have a gun handy, of course," Nick added, his words laced with irony.

Mercier nodded. "That would be wise, but it's highly unlikely you'll need it. Do you have one?"

Nick coughed a laugh. "Are you kidding? I'm a physician, an *American* residing in a foreign country. How the devil would I get a gun?"

"We've got you one," Mercier assured him. "That, plus some other things Cate might need will be in the trunk of your car."

"Well, I've shot snakes and targets, but never anything with legs. I'm not sure I could take a life." He frowned at Mercier. "Just so you know."

"Trust me, if someone starts shooting, you'll be damned glad to have the means to return fire."

"What if she refuses to go with me?" Nick asked. That was a distinct possibility. She had always resented his "hovering" as she called it. Hated it when he cautioned her about taking risks.

"She'll go," Mercier declared. "We can't take her home yet. Ganz says she shouldn't fly for that long in her condition. For her safety, we're creating a diversion to make everyone think she's on a plane back to the States."

Mercier's wife, Solange, joined them in the waiting room just as Cate's parents came in. After greeting them, the Merciers excused themselves and went in to speak with Cate.

Cate's mother, Tess Olin, an Amazon who looked scarcely older than her daughter, approached Nick. "I know this is an imposition, dear. It's not fair to ask it of you."

Yeah, but Nick knew he really had no choice. "Dr. Ganz and Cate's supervisor agree it's the best thing. I know what to watch for, can prescribe whatever she needs and conduct her therapy."

"It's the perfect solution," Rolph Olin said. He shot a look at his wife, one that warned her to stop protesting.

"I guess it does make sense," Tess said, obviously relieved. Cate's younger brother, Anderson, nodded in agreement, looking from one parent to the other, taking his cue from them as usual.

Nick could only imagine how Cate would fare if these three took over her care. The best she could hope for would be benign neglect. The worst would be another attempt on her life when she was at her most vulnerable and unprotected.

Sending Cate into whatever kind of protection program they offered would be even worse. She would probably get very little medical attention since all the damage was virtually invisible. Her condition could deteriorate in either case.

"So you'll be flying home with her?" her mother asked.

"Of course." Nick figured it wasn't exactly a lie. They would fly home eventually. "Go ahead and do whatever you have to do. I'll take good care of Cate," he assured the Olins and was somewhat mollified by Tess's tears of relief and Rolph's obvious gratitude.

They did care about her, but they were definitely not equipped to be caregivers. All their focus was on her little brother's career. Sport freaks, to the exclusion of everything else. "I promise to call you and give you progress reports."

Tess smiled up at him and gave him a motherly hug. Rolph and Anderson shook his hand. He couldn't miss the renewed hope for a love match in their eyes, a hope both he and Cate had always resented. Even his own parents had pushed that.

Their families had been friends since he and Cate were kids. His own father was a big name in sports medicine, Cate's was a world-class coach. That common interest, and living in the same town, had cemented a friendship that had grown over the years. Their folks had entertained each other frequently and even traveled together on family vacations.

Cate was three years his junior and back then it seemed to Nick that he was the only one who cared whether she reached adulthood. Totally unsupervised and absolutely fearless, Cate had dragged him into more life-threatening scrapes than he could count. Apparently, her adventurous nature hadn't changed.

He had been relieved when he finally graduated and left home for college. While still in medical school, he had married Karen, who was the antithesis of Cate in every way imaginable. The marriage had proved a serious lapse in judgment.

Though he'd continued to worry about Cate over the years, she probably hadn't given him a second thought. According to Mercier, she loved her work battling terrorism around the world. Nick shuddered to think of the danger she had faced in her job, but he did admire her for channeling all that daredevil energy into something positive. She would not take it well when she learned that outlet was now closed to her.

He knew from experience what it was like to lose the work that defined you. His left hand clenched automatically while his right barely made a fist. Even after surgery and extensive therapy, it had taken him nearly a year to accept the permanent nerve damage and resulting changes in his life.

Maybe helping Cate come to terms with this injury would give new meaning to what he had endured and accomplished. It would be better if she didn't have to face this catastrophe alone, as he had.

Tess was speaking again, her hand on his arm. "We've already told her goodbye. We didn't mention all that we discussed about you looking after her. She'll listen to you, Nick. She always did."

No, she *rarely* had listened. But Nick nodded anyway.

The Olins were not bad people. They simply didn't know how to manage anyone who wasn't in top form physically. When one of the skiers they trained suffered an injury or illness, they passed him or her off to someone who could fix it. If there was no complete comeback in the offing—and sometimes even if there was—the individual was quickly replaced by someone else to train. Right now their hopes were pinned on getting their own son, Anderson, prepared for jumping and freestyling his way through the next Winter Olympics.

No doubt they'd be off to the nearest slopes as soon as they could make arrangements. He heard them mention Austria as they turned to leave.

Nick sat in the waiting room. Mercier and Solange, a physician who worked at the hospital in Georgetown, were still in with Cate.

When he saw them exit, he joined them in the hall. "How is she?" he asked.

Solange replied, "Restless. Attempting to cope, mostly with denial. Dr. Ganz said he would release her today, but we didn't mention that. I wonder if she should stay another day or so."

There was no reason to prolong the inevitable. "So, she's aware of Ganz's prognosis?" Nick asked. They had operated to relieve the pressure on her brain from the bleeding, but the damage had been done. She had hit a rock. In addition to that, she had been deprived of oxygen a few minutes too long before they could dig her out. It was unlikely that Cate would ever fully overcome the results of her injuries. Her vision was impaired. So were her voluntary reflexes and her equilibrium. Her thought processes had been slow at first, but that had improved fairly rapidly. It was a good sign, but not good enough.

"Yes, she has been told," Solange said with a grimace.

Mercier put an arm around her shoulders as he met Nick's gaze. "I want to thank you personally for doing this, Sandro. I imagine Cate won't be easy to live with these next few months."

"I know." Boy, did he know it. Cate had not been easy to be with when she was well and happy.

Life around her had been a roller-coaster ride. Cate embraced risk. A thrill a minute and damn the danger. All that energy. That strength. Those mercurial moods and sheer physicality. One thing he had to admit, he had never felt so alive before or since being with Cate. He had tried to hold on to that zest for life she had revealed in him. Secretly, he had envied her natural exuberance and tried to embrace it.

The trick would be to turn the force and strength of Cate's energy into something that would get her through the worst of this. And to focus whatever drive he had left on her recovery.

"No one knows your address in Florence but your parents, right?"

"I moved to a larger apartment recently, so even they don't have my exact address," Nick assured him.

Mercier nodded, obviously satisfied. "We'll make certain you aren't followed when you leave here. Two of our Italian assets are already in Florence checking out your apartment and the surrounding area. They'll identify them-

selves when you arrive. Here's the information on them."
He tucked a card into Nick's breast pocket.

"That's assuming I can persuade her to go," Nick said
with a wry smile.

"I just told her she has to," Mercier declared. "Cate's
practical. She understands that."

Mercier cleared his throat and glanced at the closed
door to Cate's room. "Well, Good luck, Sandro."

"Thanks." Nick sighed. He would need it.

Mercier had told him earlier that he had three
months, at which time he needed to know whether Cate
could function in a training capacity or at a desk job
with the agency. That time frame closely coincided with
the date Nick had to report for the fellowship he'd
decided to take.

Psychiatry was a far cry from neurosurgery, but it was
one of the possibilities open to him now that he lacked the
strength and fine motor skills necessary for delicate opera-
tions. So they had three short months for Cate to reinvent
herself.

He took leave of the Merciers and went back in to speak
with Cate. She looked exhausted, barely able to stay
awake. "Hey, girl. Did they wear you out?"

"God, this is the longest day ever," she groaned. "What
are my chances of getting out of this place so I can get some
rest?"

"Pretty good, actually. You'll be staying with me for a
while," Nick said, reaching for her hand and clasping it
with his left. "Don't you dare say no. I'm looking forward
to making you my famous spaghetti."

"Oh, please," she groaned, and made a face. "Not with the olives?"

"*Black* olives now," he replied with a grin. "I've gone exotic."

She wriggled around, withdrawing her hand from his and pulling up the sheet to cover her breasts, clearly outlined by the soft cotton print.

Her gaze fastened on the window. "They shouldn't expect you to babysit me, Nick. I told them that."

"We *are* doing this," he declared. "It's all settled. No arguments."

She brushed a hand over her face. "Jack made my alternative pretty clear, but it's so not fair to you. Gives new meaning to the word imposition."

"Your mom said that, too, but it's not imposing. I volunteered for it." He managed another grin to cover the lie and flashed her the Boy Scout pledge.

"You did no such thing and we both know it." She sighed. "And what if I don't choose to be your good deed for the day?"

"I'll carry you off like the caveman I can be when you strip me down to essentials. You know I'll do it."

She laughed. "Caveman stripped down, huh?"

Nick didn't miss that fleeting expression that said she did recall him stripped. Her awareness of him as a man had always made him feel primal. Again, the old guilt over that surfaced, but he dismissed it. He made up his mind to view her as a grown woman from now on, not as the precocious kid who hit on him regularly and delighted in making him uncomfortable.

She had burst into the bathroom and seen him naked in the shower once. And stared, fascinated, amused and aroused, too, if those little breasts of hers had been any indication. It had *not* been his fault.

Her gaze shifted from heated to frustrated in the space of a heartbeat. "So when do we blow this joint? I'm sick to death of it."

Nick released the pent-up breath he'd been holding. "This afternoon looks good for me."

Her blue eyes flew wide. "Seriously? *Today?*"

She had been here for three weeks, conscious for two of them, ambulatory for one.

"They've done about all they can do here. Now comes the real work." He shot her a warning look. "You know I'll be a slave driver, don't you?"

Cate exhaled, looking incredibly weary. All the visitors today hadn't helped. Maybe she was too tired to make the trip. "If you want to wait until tomorrow, Cate, it's okay," he said.

"Not on your life. If I have to sneak out the back door dressed in this backless wonder and mooning the locals, I'll do it. You said *today*."

"Today it is. You take a short nap while I get the paperwork done. Then I'll send in a nurse to help you dress. I hope your mom brought some clothes for you. If not, I'll get you a set of scrubs to wear. Nap now," he ordered, shaking his finger at her.

She clenched her eyes shut and pulled the sheet up under her chin. "Sleeping, see? Go sign me out."

Nick reached through the railing of her bed and squeezed her foot. "See you in about an hour, twerp."

He had to get out of here before he made an idiot of himself, kissed her and promised he'd make her well despite the overwhelming odds against it.

Seeing her this way, weak, bedridden and so desperate to escape the hospital she would go with anyone, made Nick worry that maybe this wasn't going to work. What if he was too personally involved to help Cate do what she needed to do? Could he ignore all the old feelings and be professional enough?

He had left her alone when she was seventeen because he had to, but it hadn't been easy. He had put her firmly out of his reach. Now she was thirty. And a *patient,* he reminded himself sternly. Still off-limits. No way would he become involved with a patient. Not even Cate.

"The last time you wore that look I had just laid a wet one on you under the mistletoe," Cate said, laughing. "Do I still scare you, sweetheart?"

He shook his head in sheer exasperation. What the hell was he going to do with her? *That* was what scared him.

Chapter 2

Laughter proved the only weapon available as Cate fought tears of frustration and fear. She had to lick this. And who did they send to help? The man she had avoided like the plague for years.

God, why did he have to look so damn good? Who was she kidding? Even if he had gotten bald and fat, he would still be Nick, the only man she had ever pursued. And she had done that with such a wicked vengeance, ignoring his every protest, knowing that her aggressive behavior had actually pushed him away. How embarrassing was that?

What was her family thinking? Unfortunately, she could no longer tell and that was yet another source of frustration. They had always been a snap to read. Now she couldn't even grasp how they were feeling, much less pick up any of their thoughts.

Both she and Nick had known their parents hoped for an eventual love match and resented that fiercely as most teenagers would. Only she had rebelled by provoking him, daring him, making him miserable. She was sure he had seen her as a pest. She had deliberately acted like one.

Their folks had given up the matchmaking after they saw their children's lives headed down totally different paths. Nick's marriage had quelled their hopes completely. And surprisingly, had secretly devastated Cate. She hadn't even realized how much she really wanted him.

Nothing had cooled as far as she was concerned. And Nick wanted her, but obviously still felt guilty about it. Now it wasn't her age or their parents' interference, it was his ethics. It would always be something. They were just too different to get it on. She would have to curb her libido and give him a break.

Maybe he could help her recover from this injury. Not that further surgery ever could, so her neurologist had said, but if anyone could work a miracle, it would be Nick.

Couldn't he see they were all using him? That she would feel she was, too, if she let him look after her? He'd insist on it anyway, though. Nick was like that, a born healer, Dr. Responsibility. And stubborn as the day was long. Worse than she was, if that was possible.

God, she did not want to go to Italy with him.

Cate wanted to cry, but she wouldn't. This would pass, this weakness, this dizzy feeling, the horrendous headaches, nausea and rapid mood swings. Nick would know how to fix it all. He always knew how to fix things. Leaky faucets, faulty spark plugs, people's brains. He was her best chance to beat this.

Surely she could stand the embarrassment of being with him if he could teach her how to overcome her injuries. He didn't seem to be holding a grudge after all this time. He hadn't ever, bless his heart.

Their paths had crossed occasionally when she had gone home to Elizabethtown, New York, for a visit and he happened to be there, too. It was impossible to avoid one another in a town that size. Their brief greetings had been understandably cool. Barely polite, but never hostile. It was just that she hadn't wanted to set off any errant sparks and knew he had felt the same.

They wouldn't do any sparking this time, either, and in spite of her teasing just now, she would see to that. Except for her age, all the old reasons they shouldn't act on what they felt were still alive and kicking, magnified now by the intervening years and added to by the present situation. He had been right then and he was right now.

Her ruminations went on and on, preventing sleep. Before she knew it the nurse had come to help her dress. That proved no small feat since it involved sitting up, then trying to stand while the room spun. Not fun. She managed to get her clothes on before the nausea overcame her and she had to throw up. After that, she settled in the wheelchair to wait.

"Ready to go?" Nick asked as he breezed in, still looking like a cool million. She closed her eyes against the sight, but the image stuck. Oh, man, what eye candy!

He had always turned her on, even as a kid. As a fully mature man, he set her hormones bouncing big-time.

He had this intense look about him, riveting brown eyes and a strong jaw that gave him a determined, capable-of-anything appearance. His body had filled out, grown more muscular and less rangy. She tried not to imagine what it would feel like to have him hold her, to have him love her like no one else ever would.

He approached and she caught a whiff of his after-shave. Smelled like heaven must, she thought, realizing that part of the essence was Nick himself. Good ol' phero-mones.

"I'll take it from here," he said to the nurse who was about to wheel her out.

They left by a little-used exit. Cate noted a gray Volvo parked right behind the dark blue Audi Nick guided her to. She recognized Danielle Michaels, one of her fellow agents, in the Volvo's driver's seat and another, Vanessa Senate, riding shotgun.

"Hi, guys!" she called. Danielle waved at her and gave her a thumbs-up. Van smiled, too. They had been in for brief visits, along with her other teammates. God, she missed them. She missed work.

"What are they doing here?" she asked Nick as he helped her out of the wheelchair and into the comfy pas-senger seat of his Audi.

"Escorting us out of town," Nick said. "Sort of like an honor guard."

Cate fastened her seat belt. "Trust them to make a big deal out of nothing."

"Hey, it's a big day for you. They wanted to throw a keg party, but I declined on your behalf."

"Meanie."

"Yeah, well, I recall your fondness for suds and I don't think you're quite up to a hangover." He pushed a lever and reclined her seat. "Just relax and don't try to view the passing scenery. Might make you carsick. Try to sleep if you can. Want something to help?"

"Nope. No more pills. If I get the urge to upchuck, I'll let you know so you can pull over." She did as he instructed, well aware of the effect visual motion had on her even when she was sitting still.

They rode for a while with only the soft music from the radio filling the silence. Cate couldn't sleep.

She kept stealing glances at Nick through her lowered lashes. "Better get this out of the way now, I guess. Do you forgive me?" she asked, unable to stand the question foremost on her mind.

"For what?" he asked.

Cate chuckled. "Hitting on you when you couldn't hit back. I knew you wanted to."

"Shut up," he said playfully. "You did drive me crazy."

"I know. Actually, I read your mind. Knew exactly what you were thinking. I told you so then, but you didn't believe me."

He smiled. "Yeah, well, you *were* definitely a little witch."

"You still don't believe it, do you?"

He shook his head. "You might have Mercier and the government snowed with that psychic claptrap, but *I* know how you do it."

"Do you really?" She would never convince him. She hadn't exactly kept her ability a secret from him, but hadn't offered any proof of it, either. She had welcomed his skepticism. Not fair, maybe, but a girl had to use everything available to get things going. Or end it when it was time.

But what did that matter now? She couldn't do it anymore. Her "gift" had always been there and very early on she had found it proved much more useful if she kept it to herself. Nobody had believed her anyway unless she demonstrated it and then it seemed to scare them off.

Only after she heard about the COMPASS team and applied for it had she been totally upfront about what she could do. Telepathy had become a large part of her job, maybe the most important skill she had. Was that why Mercier no longer wanted her as a field agent? Did he realize she had lost it? And if he did, how could he know it wasn't a temporary loss? How could she?

Somehow, though, she needed Nick to know she had been inside his head, to believe it now. Maybe she just needed to convince herself it had been real and that it could be again. "You had some serious stuff going on in that mind of yours."

"Like worrying about a jail term if I let you have your way with me," he said lightly. "Did that register at all?"

"Yeah, I got that, and I'm apologizing for it, okay? Can we be friends again, Nick? Can we put all that behind us and just…get on with this?" God, could she sound more needy?

"Good friends, always," he agreed with an emphatic

nod. "We've never been other than that, Catie. Just relax and don't worry about a thing."

Cate couldn't let it go. It sounded too pat, too easy. "So you're not still mad about it, even a little?"

"Of course not. Can't you read my mind and tell?" he teased.

No, not even a little bit. She'd get it back, though. She had to. God, it was like a giant hole in her awareness, that missing ability. Yet another handicap she had to overcome. She missed it as much as she would any of her other five senses. But Nick couldn't help her with this.

She needed to understand precisely what her other handicaps were. "Nick, could you explain it to me and dumb it down to layman's terms? Dr. Ganz told me everything, but I didn't get much after his initial message of doom and gloom."

Nick sighed and renewed his grip on the steering wheel as if bracing himself for something unpleasant.

"All right. Hitting that rock caused bruising and trauma to your brain. When there's a sharp blow to the head like that, the bruising and the damage to the internal tissue and blood vessels is due to a something we call coup-countercoup."

"Sounds like a double whammy," she said, trying to conceal her fear.

"Exactly. The bruise directly related to trauma at the site of the injury is the coup. When the brain jolts backward, it can hit the skull on the opposite side and cause a bruise called the countercoup. The impact of the brain against the sides of the skull can cause a sort of tearing of the lining, tissues and vessels. The result of that can be bruising or swelling of the brain and internal bleeding. That's why Ganz did the surgery, to relieve the pressure from the bleed."

"I see." Cate ran a finger over the healing scar and the stubble of hair growing in around it.

Nick continued. "Some injuries aren't so bad and the symptoms and disabilities disappear over time, while some are severe and may result in permanent impairment."

"So how severe is mine?" she asked, hating how scared she sounded. But she had to know. "It must be pretty bad."

He glanced at her and tried to smile. "Well, certainly not minor, but you're still very lucky. All your motor functions seem to be working, if a little slowly. They will get better, though."

So maybe she'd get her extra faculty back in time, she thought, hanging on to the hope.

"What's your main concern here, Cate?" he asked.

"Going back to work. Why is Mercier so dead set against that?"

He shrugged. "The seizures would be my guess. You had several immediately after they brought you in. Grand mal type." He hesitated for a few seconds. "Those could happen again at any time in the future with little or no warning. You can see how that would hamper you as a field agent and put others at risk."

"Ah. Well, suppose I took antiseizure meds?"

"Could impair cognitive functions you'd need to have sharp on the job."

"Space me out you mean?" She swallowed hard and closed her eyes. "Okay, that's enough. I get the picture, though I don't necessarily agree that I'm a lost cause."

Somehow she'd think of something to get around Mercier's main objection. Maybe have a number of EEG's over the next few months and prove there was no longer a threat of seizures. She hadn't had a single seizure since she woke up. Mercier would be convinced eventually.

She could hear just fine, no numbness, her taste and smell seemed okay. But occasional double vision and the loss of her sixth sense worried her. She felt lost without the telepathy.

She couldn't talk to Nick about the absence of that skill if he didn't even believe she had it to begin with, so she deliberately changed the subject.

"My moving in with you won't mess up anything you've got going, will it? With someone else, I mean."

"No, I'm not involved at the moment. How about you?"

"No. There's no one," she answered, even as she suddenly realized there probably never would be—nothing serious anyway. She compared every man she met to Nick. Why hadn't she noticed before that she was automatically doing that?

She ran her thumb beneath the seat belt where it pressed against her chest. "So this Boy-Scout deed of yours. It wasn't really your choice, was it?"

He hesitated just a beat too long. "I care about you, Cate. I want you to recover to the maximum extent and also make sure you can deal with whatever is *not* possible."

She sat up straight and glared at him. "Well, that sounds depressing as hell and pretty damned pessimistic. What do you mean?"

He punched off the radio. "You do understand that

full recovery is probably out of the question? I know Ganz told you that. Solange Mercier affirmed it and I have to agree."

"Bull, you don't *have* to," she scoffed, sitting back and crossing her arms over her chest. "I don't care what any of you say, I can whip this, Nick. If you're giving up before we get started, I don't need your so-called help!"

Rising fury had her close to hyperventilating. Her face felt hot as hell and her nails bit into her palms. She recognized the unwarranted anger and knew the heightened emotion was a product of her injury. She deliberately tamped it down. It was a good sign that she could control it, Cate decided with a firm nod. Progress already.

"I'm not giving up, Cate," Nick told her, shaking his head. "Only trying to prepare you."

"I *am* prepared," she said, biting off the words, determined not to unleash her feelings and give him the notion that they were uncontrollable. "I'm fully prepared to do whatever is necessary and then some. I will get back to top speed and I'll do it in three months. You watch me."

He shot her a look that contained no sympathy whatsoever. She hadn't expected that. She had thought he would cajole, maybe tease or argue just to strengthen her determination. Instead, he focused again on the highway. "I see we'll have to work on your acceptance of limitations." His voice was matter-of-fact. "That will be your greatest challenge."

He turned the radio on again. Cate watched him for a few minutes, wondering what was going on in that mind of his right now. God, she wished she could read him the

way she used to. But the gift was gone, buried under the
snow in the Bernese Alps, along with her balance and
depth perception. Maybe forever.

What if he was right? She would be so screwed.

No. She could *not* let herself think that way, even for a
second. With enough hard work and dedication, Cate knew
she would come out of this whole. She would do anything,
go to any lengths, to make that happen.

For now, she was determined to enjoy the moment. Or
rather the hours it would take to reach Florence. She had
traveled very little in Europe when she hadn't been in a
hurry to get where she was going. She decided to stay
awake as Nick drove over the Simplon Pass from Switzerland into Italy. When traveling by train or air there was
little to see but the insides of enormously long tunnels or
the topside of clouds. So this scenery was new to her and
distracting, thank goodness.

The snow-capped peaks were nothing new, but the sight
of them, up close or at a distance, always filled her with
awe. Even the memory of being trapped beneath all that
snow so recently didn't cause the view to pale. "I love it
over here," she muttered. "So beautiful."

"You should be sleeping," Nick replied. "Are the curves
getting to you? I figured this would be better than the
tunnel."

"Claustrophobic, are we?" she asked with a grin.

"No, actually it's the lack of lines on the road that separate the traffic going in opposite directions. A little un-
nerving." He paused. "You feeling okay?"

"Not as bad as you'd think. And I don't want to miss

all this." She fluttered her fingers against the car window. "Fantastic."

The faint threat of nausea and the constant blurring bothered her, but she found she could take brief looks, close her eyes for a while and then open them to something totally new.

There were gorgeous waterfalls, some even channeled over the road by special concrete structures that also lent protection against avalanches. She shivered at the very thought of avalanches. But what were the chances of being caught in two within the month? She quickly dismissed the thought.

Chalets had sprung up in places where it seemed no human should or could live. Real *Heidi* country, she thought with a smile, recalling the poignant story from her childhood. "Look! There are some sheep!"

"Goats," he argued, correcting her with a laugh.

"Okay, so I don't see all the details. I will. And I'll come back here soon and ski that slope," she promised herself out loud. She noticed the look on Nick's face as she said it. He didn't think she'd be able to face it, or maybe didn't think she ought to try.

"Hey, you get thrown, you get up and get back on the horse," she explained.

"Not if the outlaws are shooting at you," he reminded her. "Then you scramble for cover, which is precisely what you're doing."

"You're a cautious man, Nicky," she said with a chuckle. "You always were."

"Is that your Latin for *coward?*" he asked with a smile.

"No, of course not," she assured him. "It's just that you spend too much time looking and never, ever leap."

He inclined his head in agreement. "Maybe that's why I'm not the one running for my life."

Chapter 3

Even though it extended travel time, Nick had opted for the less-congested autostrada instead of taking the A1 main artery leading to the city. That made it easier to determine whether anyone had followed them. No one had, he was certain.

They arrived late in the day, just as the sun was throwing its golden glow over the city. He didn't wake Cate to see it. As eager as he was to share the beauty of Florence with her, that would have to wait. Brunelleschi's beautiful, striped dome shone in the distance like a beacon leading him to the area that was his temporary home.

He loved Italy and especially old world Firenze, even though the Sandro family originally hailed from Rome. When he'd first arrived, he had considered making the move permanent. He had even been offered a position on staff where he was attending the seminars. But his plans were already made for the fellowship and he hadn't liked the idea of taking the easy way out. Besides, he was admittedly addicted to fast-lane living and rather spoiled when it came to amenities not available anywhere else but the States.

When they reached his building, Nick parked in front, half on the cobbled sidewalk, as everyone did. He woke Cate, helped her from the car and ushered her inside to the lift that would take them to his second-floor apartment.

His bedroom was the larger of the two, but fronted the street, so he guided her to the guest room. It looked rather spartan, but he figured she was too tired to notice anyway. Tomorrow he would see about fixing it up for her. She collapsed immediately without so much as a good-night.

Too wired to go to bed so early in the evening, he went to the kitchen, heated a can of soup and made himself a ham sandwich.

The two agents Mercier had contacted in Florence came by after darkness fell, supplying the proper password so that Nick could identify them as being who they claimed to be.

One was a portly little guy in his early thirties, sporting a neat moustache and wearing an expensively tailored suit. The other looked slightly older, tall, built like a wrestler and dressed more casually. Both were Italian, probably former military, judging by their bearing.

Their English was fairly fluent, but out of politeness,

since this was their country, Nick switched easily to the Italian his grandmother had required that he learn.

Tosseli and Giacomo reassured him they would remain on watch from the rooms they pointed out in the building across the street. Anytime Nick and Cate went out, he was supposed to ring them up and let them know. The telltale bulges beneath Tosseli's coat and Giacomo's loose-tailed shirt assured Nick they were loaded for bear.

Despite Nick's aversion to firearms, these he didn't mind. If someone did come after Cate, he wanted all the backup he could get.

After their watchdogs left, Nick went to bed. He fought with dreams of Cate all night long, the same dreams he had battled when he had left her to go away to school. Hot dreams. Then there were the nightmares about there being no one to save her from herself. But the hot dreams dominated.

He knew he couldn't keep dwelling on the past this way or he'd go nuts. Cate had made it perfectly clear she just wanted to be friends now, nothing else. She had even felt easy enough with him to tease him about those early years.

How could they be anything else but friends? He was in no frame of mind to embark on a relationship. He had lost his livelihood and whether he would succeed in his next position was anybody's guess. There was the fellowship coming up, more training. Analysis. Setting up practice, if that's what he decided to do in the new specialty. What if he found he hated psychiatry? Yet another field? More training? For the first time in his life, his future was uncertain.

And even if he were already settled into something career-wise, what about Cate? She had some huge life changes down the road whether she accepted that fact or not. He wasn't sure he could help her much past the immediate recovery phase.

It seemed he needed to work on acceptance as badly as she did because he still wanted her, so badly that he might settle for something as temporary as a one-night stand.

He made up his mind to retreat into doctor mode for the duration. He would *not* let this get out of hand. It could only hurt both of them.

By morning, he had his resolve firmly in place.

"Breakfast," Nick announced, placing a tray on the table next to her bed.

Last night she had insisted on using the walker for balance to get herself to the bathroom and back. He knew that changing her clothes must have been difficult, but her determination had won out. The T-shirt she wore to sleep in was on inside out, he noted. Either she hadn't noticed or hadn't had the energy left to fix it.

She pushed up in bed, closing her eyes momentarily and swaying a little. He watched her swallow hard several times and take a deep, shuddering breath. It took her nearly a full minute to recover from the sudden movement.

"Take it slowly next time. Give your senses a chance to catch up. Your body's doing one thing, your brain is registering something else. Disorienting, I know, but you'll learn to adjust and compensate."

Cate shot him a nasty look and crossed her arms over her chest. "I'm fine. So what's to eat?"

He took the tray and placed it in her lap. "Egg, toast and coffee. Decaf cappuccino."

She wrinkled her nose. "You know I *hate* decaf anything! The least you can do is bring me high-test. I'll make it myself in the morning."

"There's juice, too, if you don't want cappuccino." He pulled a chair next to her bed to join her, and reached for his own cup of regular coffee.

She beat him to it, laughing when she tasted it. "I *knew* you wouldn't drink the fake stuff. Or the sweet stuff! This one is mine!"

Nick sighed. She was going to be a handful, but he had known that going into this. "Have it your way." He picked up her juice and took a sip. "Soon as you finish, we'll get you up and running, so to speak."

"A jog around the block? Just what the doctor ordered and I see you're dressed for it. I hope you've removed all the local statuary to prevent collision damage." She winked. "Though I wouldn't mind running into *The David.* What a bod!"

"Joke all you want. I know this balance thing is driving you crazy. We're going to improve that, but don't expect miracles by this afternoon, okay?"

She nodded, then dug into the egg, making a face as she did it. "It might take a week or so. I'm good with that."

He remained silent, unwilling to burst her bubble and not even certain he could if he tried. She obviously needed time to come to terms with the truth of her condition.

"Great coffee," she told him. "I want a refill after my shower."

Nick took the tray and set it on the nightstand. "You have to let me help you with that, Cate. Can't have you falling and breaking something."

"Help with the coffee, yes. With the shower, no," she declared. "I can do this by myself, Nick."

"Cate…"

"I *will* be careful," she promised, giving him her stubborn grin. "No chance in hell you're gonna see me naked after all these years."

"Well, that's a relief." It was. He had seen her naked once, poised on the pier near his family's cabin on the Waxahatchee River, about to dive. A nymph at dawn, all golden and surreal, too beautiful for words. The image was branded on his mind forever.

He stood and picked up the breakfast tray, shoving his chair out of the way with one foot. "If you run into trouble, I think I can stand what gravity must have done to you in your old age. Holler if you need me. And take your time. Move very carefully, okay?"

"Aye, sir!" She saluted.

It was all he could do to leave the room. In spite of that, he did feel relieved that she was taking charge of the more intimate tasks necessary. He could only imagine what seeing her naked with warm water sluicing over her would do to his own equilibrium.

Cate managed to make it to the bathroom. The aluminum walker surrounded her on three sides, providing the stability she needed. She slid it carefully forward on the tiled floor, afraid to lift it for fear she would tilt sideways and fall.

The step-in shower was easy to access and operate. She made quick work of it, leaning on the walker to steady herself. Then she grabbed a towel, dried off and pulled Nick's terry robe off the nearby hook. Snuggled inside it, she raised one lapel to her nose and smiled as she inhaled his scent.

Feeling refreshed and enjoying her successful stab at independence, Cate headed for the sink. She wiped off the steam and took a good look at herself in the mirror. If she stood real still, there was only one of her looking back.

"Now that wasn't so hard, was it?" she asked her reflection. Man, she looked pathetic. No worry that Nick would want to kindle anything with her looking like *this*. Not that she was even entertaining the thought.

The truth was, she would always love Nick, but she knew love was not enough to surmount all their differences. She could never have been a doctor's wife with all that entailed, the social obligations, the sacrifice of her own goals. And he could hardly be expected to enjoy life as a husband to someone like her. Not Nick the worrier.

Nope, that would never have worked then and wouldn't work now. A silly girl's pipe dreams, that's all. Time to put them away, file them under misty memories and what-might-have-beens.

She reached up and raked her wet hair back with one hand. Needed lightening, she thought with a sigh. Needed a cut. They had chopped out a chunk, then shaved it down to the scalp around the site of her surgery, a round gap of half-inch stubble that looked horrible unless she did a sort of comb-over. The word made her grin at herself in the mirror.

She plundered shamelessly in the drawers of the bathroom cabinet and came up with a pair of scissors. Maybe she could go punk.

If she couldn't control anything else in her life right now, at least she could take charge of her appearance.

Confident she could look no worse than she did now, Cate grabbed up a comb, separated a section of hair and began to snip. She could do this.

What was she doing in there? Nick paced the hallway, waiting for her to come out. The water was off, had been for ten minutes. Maybe she was using the bathroom. He wasn't about to storm in and embarrass her.

"You all right, Cate?" he called.

"No…" He heard her drawn-out moan. Pain? Something clattered to the floor.

"I'm coming in," he warned.

The moment the door opened, Nick gasped.

She turned to him, tears in her eyes and sobbed. "It… It's *awful!*"

He took it in. Long pale hanks of hair littered the sink and floor. The scissors lay open, next to the faucet. His hairbrush and the small hand dryer had tumbled to the floor. Cate was grasping the bars of the walker in a white knuckled grip. Wet hair stood straight out from her head in uneven lengths.

"Oh, Catie," he groaned.

"Fix it," she pleaded.

He had never heard her sound so desperate about anything. She certainly had never worried much about her looks. Hadn't had to. She was a natural beauty.

He went to her and took her in his arms, the bars of the walker between them, a reminder of why she was here. Gently, he patted her shoulders and barely stopped himself from kissing her on the head. "It'll be okay. Let's go where you can sit down."

Patiently, moving at turtle's speed, he helped her out of the bathroom and into the club chair by the window in the bedroom. Then he retrieved the comb, scissors and dryer.

Good Lord, what had he gotten himself into? Should he call a stylist? Who the heck would make house calls? He didn't know anyone else who could do this. At least not nearby and not on a Sunday.

Though she wasn't vain, Cate had always spent a fortune on her haircuts. She had told him once that a good haircut saved money and time because it required so little in-between care. Her straight, part in the middle, all one-length style suited her perfectly and hadn't changed a bit since she was a kid. Until now.

Well, hell, he was a surgeon. Or had been. Surely he could manage to even up a few strands of hair. Cate was unduly upset by this little tragedy and he couldn't have that.

"We'll have this straightened out in no time," he assured her. "Just sit there, close your eyes and be patient."

She sniffled. "I thought I could…"

"I know, I know. Actually, it's not that bad," he said,

hiding a grimace. Actually, it was terrible. She had butchered it. He might not know much about hairstyles, but he could surely make it better than it was now.

He tried to remember what he'd seen the stylists do to women's hair in the shop where he had his cut. It bothered him that he wasn't nearly as observant as he'd always thought. His right hand worked better at this than he had imagined it would, but little strength was required to separate sections of hair and hold it for cutting. The movements of his left were as precise as ever.

After about ten minutes, he laid the scissors down, fluffed what was left of Cate's hair out with his fingers and plugged in the hair dryer. He sort of rolled the brush at the crown of her head, giving her hair some puff. Unfortunately, that was about all he could recall a stylist doing. He smoothed down the rest around her face.

She sat stiffly, eyes tightly shut, her breathing sounding about as ragged as her hair had looked.

The result was a fringed pixie cut that looked oddly endearing on Cate, at least to Nick. He missed the silken flow that used to entice him to stroke it. Good. Now he'd no longer have to deal with that particular temptation. Besides, this new wash-and-go hairdo would be much more practical for her right now.

He gave her shorn hair a final ruffle. "Finished! Girl, I think I missed my calling. You are gorgeous."

She opened her eyes and looked up at him. "I overreacted, didn't I? Crying over my hair is not rational behavior. I'm much worse off than I thought."

Nick tweaked her chin. "Give yourself a break, would

you? Women obsess over their looks all the time." He leaned closer and winked. "Want to hear a secret? Men do it, too. It's allowed. Now, you want to see?"

She braced her hands on the arms of the chair and got to her feet. Nick led her back into the bathroom, anxious to see whether his efforts would rouse a new spate of tears. Or maybe outright hysteria.

Cate was kind. She smiled, reaching up to flick the bangs, then tug them into some sort of order only she could see. "Not too bad. Now what can you do about these dark circles under my eyes?"

Nick's breath gusted out in a wave of relief. "Feed you regularly and see that you get enough sleep and exercise."

Her direct gaze met his in the mirror's reflection. "Thanks, Nicky," she whispered. "For everything. You didn't have to do…all this. Take me in, feed me, do my hair…"

"Sure I did," he said, hoping she never learned how he had argued against taking her on. "You'd do as much for me, wouldn't you?"

She nodded. "Could…could we get on with whatever you do have in mind for rehab?"

Nick shrugged. "Don't you want a day to rest up before we start, maybe tour the apartment, sit outside on the balcony and watch the tourists? Not many come this way, but the locals are interesting. Most are attending church at this hour, but later it gets pretty lively out there."

She clicked her tongue, impatient. "I don't have time to watch people!"

He laughed, relieved that her mood had switched. "Then get your britches on and let's go to work."

"Where?" she asked, looking altogether too excited, probably expecting a full-scale workout, complete with hand-to-hand combat. Unless she had acquired some patience in the intervening years, he had his work cut out for him.

"I've set up in the lounge. I want to do some basic evaluation, then start with hand-eye coordination exercises and build from there. I know they did tests in the hospital, but I need to judge the extent of the injury for myself. And for you, of course. First, we'll define exactly which parts of your brain are affected, then construct the actual therapy so that other parts can take over and learn new tricks."

"Got it," she said with apparent enthusiasm. "So get out of here and let me get dressed." Her blue eyes twinkled with mischief. "Unless you want to observe me and see how my coordination works with that."

"Don't think I'm not tempted." He teased her back with a fake leer. It felt a little too real.

She gave him a push. "Get *out* of here!"

Her moods were very pronounced and changed too rapidly with too little cause, he noted. Similar to bipolar symptoms. Could be that she was merely nervous about being with him in a doctor/patient situation. That couldn't be any easier for her than it was for him. Something to watch, at any rate.

Cate examined the navy sweats he'd left for her to wear, the matching hoodie, white T-shirt and a pair of his sneakers. Those would be too big for her, but not by much and he'd provided thick socks. Walking would be easier with shoes. She had the changes of clothing that her mother had bought, but they were dressy outfits, as useless as the fancy low-heeled pumps and slick-soled flats.

Cate wondered what had happened to the bag she had with her at the ski resort. They would have to shop for clothes for her, but not today.

He came back fifteen minutes later. She was dressed, but exhausted now and lying on her back across the bed. He sat in the chair and crossed his arms over his chest. "Tire out real easily, huh?"

She groaned. "Weak as a kitten! Couldn't even manage the socks and shoes. Tell me this is temporary."

"It is, but you can't rush it too much."

"Funny, you never realize how wonderful it is to be normal until you're not."

He picked up one of the socks and Cate lifted her foot. "You were actually *normal?* When was that?" he asked, joking as he slid the sock on.

Years worth of adrenaline-powered action scenes and arduous training ops flashed through her mind like a high-speed slide show. "When I was with you. When you told me what to do. How to be," she answered without thinking.

Their eyes met. He drew a finger down the side of her ankle, then held her foot flat against his chest, caressing it.

Her breath caught in her throat as the warmth of his gaze registered fully. She clenched her eyes shut against the heat in his.

He gently lowered her foot, then released it. When she

opened her eyes, the heat was gone and so was Nick. He had closed the door between them. Or maybe she had done that with her response.

Chapter 4

"Stupid," she muttered to herself. "Your hair's a mess. Your whole *life* is a mess. For God's sake, don't wreck *his*."

Cate knew she had to face him, but it was a good half hour before she got up the energy to put on the shoes and venture out of the room. The aluminum walker gave her a sense of safety. She took it one slow step at a time down the hall. Once she had her bearings, it was a bit easier to stay on course and speed up. Her legs felt steadier, stronger, not wobbly. Compensating already, she thought, encouraged. She flexed her leg muscles and that felt good. Much of the weakness was the result of being bedridden for so long.

Maybe she was thinking about it too much. Surely she

had some automatic reflexes that would kick in if she gave them a chance. Explore, she told herself and tried to forget about her clumsy balance and focus on touring the apartment.

Kitchen first. Noting the simple decor and how it reflected Nick's taste, or lack of it, she smiled at two whimsical fridge magnets depicting cartoon-like doctors. Where the devil had those come from? Her hand trailed the wall with its textured finish made to look like real plaster.

Yeah, she found she was more sure on her feet when she didn't consciously work at it and worry about it. Hope ratcheted up another notch. Still, however, her vision wavered and doubled whenever she moved her head quickly or tried too hard to focus on one thing. Spirits high in spite of that, she went to find Nick and tell him what she'd discovered.

She heard his voice as she approached the open doorway of his lounge and stopped there. He had his back to her and was on his cell phone, speaking in rapid Italian.

"No, I haven't seen him since you two were here last night. He was in the apartment across the way at eleven. Or was that you?" Silence for a full minute. "Yes, I understand. No, we won't go out." He replaced the phone.

"What's up?" Cate demanded from the doorway.

Nick held up a finger, signaling her to wait. He punched in a number on his cell phone. "Mercier? We've got a problem. One of your men seems to have disappeared."

A long silence ensued as he listened, then he spoke again, his voice betraying his relief. "You're sure? This is the guy?"

Cate almost interrupted.

"Thank God," he said. "You'll keep us informed, right? If you're mistaken, I want to know it the minute you do. Got that? Okay, I'm good with it. We'll be fine." He paused. "You could have called immediately."

He closed the phone and gestured impatiently with his free hand, then took a deep breath and made yet another call, switching again to Italian. "Giacomo? Mercier says they got the shooter. Maybe Tosseli got the word and left. You're still on, right? No one's reassigned you?"

For a long time, he said nothing, then finally responded. "Let me know what you find out."

He crooked a finger, signaling Cate to come in. Nodding, he offered her a halfhearted smile as he said a perfunctory goodbye and rang off.

"They've got the man who caused the avalanche. Found him hiding out in one of the cabins with a rifle. No admission that he was after you, but Mercier says he's a known gun for hire."

"Great. But you're still worried about Tosseli, aren't you?" Cate demanded. "You don't really think he got the word it was over."

"Mercier didn't contact him, Cate. It's not over. The man they arrested was an assassin, obviously hired by someone to kill you. Whoever did that has had three weeks to find out you're still alive and make other arrangements."

Cate had figured as much. She had to get on the inside of this investigation somehow and do her part to determine who was after her. But how could she do that stuck here in Florence doing exercises and mind games with Nick?

"Tosseli's gone," he said, pounding a fist in his palm. "They were both on duty last night. Before dawn, Tosseli went out for their breakfast, intending to come by and check in with me. He never turned up here and he didn't make it back to their rooms."

Nick began to pace. "Gives me a bad feeling, Catie. He didn't seem the type to play hooky."

Cate didn't like it, either. Mercier was damn careful in choosing responsible and well-qualified agents abroad because they often had to act independently and use their own judgment. "Well, at least Jack got the shooter."

Nick's lips tightened and he shook his head. "Yes, but he was only a hired gun."

"Yeah, I get that. But we weren't followed out of Switzerland. Danielle and Van would have seen to that. They're good, Nick. Very, very good at what they do. So is Jack Mercier."

Nick didn't look at all mollified. "Still…someone could have guessed I brought you here. Or might have overheard something at the hospital." The question in his eyes prodded her to answer. "First thing they'd do is take out the guards, right?"

Cate nodded. "How are we fixed for defense?" she asked, trying to sound calm so he wouldn't panic. She'd never seen him freak, but this was so out of Nick's realm, he might do that.

"We should call Mercier back and see what we need to do about this." He unzipped a small duffel and was plundering through it. Cate's eyebrows rose when he pulled out a 9 mm pistol and checked the load.

She grabbed for it, but he held it away from her. "Nick! Give me that before you shoot one of us," she demanded. "You don't know a damn thing about guns!"

"I do, too, and I can shoot," he assured her, tucking it into his belt.

"At least put it in the back," she said with a chuckle. "You have no butt to speak of, but what's in front, you might not want to live without."

"This is nothing to laugh about, Cate." Nick paid no attention to her advice about the weapon, just grabbed the small bag and headed out of the room. She followed, the walker clunking as she hurried to catch up.

"What are you doing?" she demanded when he reached the kitchen and began tossing pill bottles into the bag. He jerked open the fridge, grabbed a bottle of water and added it.

"We're getting out of here. You can manage to ride another hour or so. I know of a villa where we can stay that's out in the boonies." He packed a small round of cheese and a bag of crackers, then zipped the bag shut and slung it over his shoulder.

"We can't leave!" she argued, gripping the walker, fully aware that she wasn't in prime mobility mode. No way could she run if the need arose. She couldn't even walk straight.

"If someone's after you and knows you're here, then you need to be somewhere else. That simple. So let's go."

"What about Giacomo?" she asked. "Don't you need to call him and let him know? Don't you trust him?"

"Not with your life I don't."

Maybe Nick was right, she thought. Agents could be turned, and she didn't know these men.

"No one's going to know. We can go out the old servants' entrance to the alley. My bike's parked in the laundry room downstairs."

Cate laughed out loud. "You want us to run away on a *bicycle?*"

"Motorcycle," he said. "Just a few blocks to the rental car agency. If someone did follow us, they'd recognize the Audi."

Cate sighed. He was all set to play James Bond. She could see it in his determined expression, in his decisive movements, in his take-charge attitude. "This is insane! We don't know what happened to Tosseli. Maybe he just got mugged. Or he could have been hit by a car. There could be any number of reasons he's not where he's supposed to be."

Nick turned her around, walker and all, and guided her down the hallway.

Should she insist on staying here and facing the threat if there actually was one? It made much more sense than haring off into the countryside. But she didn't suppose they would be any more vulnerable there than they would here. Besides that, this was a side of Nick she had never seen before and it intrigued her. Why not let him have his fun?

A motorcycle ride wouldn't kill her and if there actually was someone stalking her here in Florence, a change in location would keep Nick out of the line of fire.

She stopped him at the bedroom door and went inside.

There, she fished her cell phone and wallet out of her purse and tucked them into the hoodie's pockets. "Okay, let's go."

His frown told her that he had just realized how cumbersome it would be, getting her down the stairs with the walker.

"All right," he said, worrying his forehead with his thumb and forefinger. "I guess we'll have to go out front and take the elevator."

"Nope, the back stairs. I'm sure there's a railing, right? You can go in front of me in case I get dizzy."

"You're sure?" he asked, ushering her to the door, his hand to her back. She left the walker and they proceeded slowly down the narrow, dimly lit servants' stairs.

Just before they reached the bottom, he stopped cold, causing her to bump into his back. "My God!" he whispered, sounding horrified.

Cate looked over his shoulder. A body lay across the bottom three steps and the tinny smell of blood rose up the stuffy staircase. "Tosseli?" she asked in a hushed voice.

"No," he whispered back as he crouched and put his fingers to the man's neck. "It's Giacomo. Dead."

Okay, now things were getting serious. Whoever had killed Giacomo had probably killed Tosseli, too, unless he was in on this. At any rate, somebody was out there waiting for her and Nick to emerge. They wouldn't have left the body here if they expected an escape out the back way. They figured she would need to use the elevator in front.

She placed a firm hand on Nick's shoulder. "You've seen bodies before, Nicky. Get over it." At least the killer wasn't waiting down here. No room to hide.

"He's been knifed!"

Cate glanced back up the stairs. Nick's apartment was secure enough to prevent forced entry, but it wasn't bombproof. She shook his shoulder. "Listen to me, Nick. Stand up, step over the body and let's get out of here." She reached around his waist and drew the gun from his belt and slipped off the safety. "Don't argue. Do exactly as I say. This is my O.R. and I'm chief surgeon on this op, got that?"

"Long as the patient lives," he muttered, offering no objection to her lifting his weapon. "Sorry about the shock."

"Forget it." She fought the vertigo and a galloping case of nausea, stepped around him at the bottom landing. "Get your wheels."

He nodded and complied, rolling out an ancient vehicle that made her groan. "What the hell?"

"She might not look like much, but she can fly. No helmets, so we'll have to be careful," he warned. Now there was the Nick she knew.

"Honey, careful can get us killed. Go ahead. Climb on and get ready."

She cracked open the back door and peered in both directions, taking care to pause for a second whenever she moved her head. Apparently it took at least that space of time for her brain to catch up and register what she saw. As long as she remained still, she could see fairly well.

There was no one out there and no nooks and crannies for anyone to hide in. It looked to be smooth sailing, at least to the end of the alley. God only knew what they would encounter when they reached the street.

She opened the door wide, then felt her way gingerly to the back of the bike and climbed on behind Nick. "I hope you can drive this sucker."

"Like the wind," he promised. "You okay, Catie?"

"I'm a head case, always was," she told him with a laugh. "Yeah, I'll be fine. When you hit the street, give her all she's got."

"Don't be careful," he muttered as if reminding himself as he reached for the key.

Cate gripped his belt with her free hand and braced her gun hand against his side. She got her footing and locked her thighs around his.

They blasted out of the building like a shot, bumping over the cobbles in a bone-jarring dash for the street. Her vision blurred with the vibration.

He swung out onto the street, narrowly missing a green vehicle. Its horn whined an anemic reprimand as they flew down the street.

Cate peeked over Nick's shoulder and squinted. At the end of the block, a tall figure swiftly crouched, arms straight, aiming a handgun directly at them. The image shifted into two fuzzy ones.

Without thought, she propped her forearm against Nick's extended elbow and fired in between the double images, then at each in turn. Six rounds should have hit the shooter *somewhere* even though her vision was a bit screwed. Okay, a *lot* screwed. At least the target fell.

Nick zoomed around the body and picked up speed. The hairs on the back of her neck stood straight out. Her back tingled, expecting a bullet to zap her any second.

Adrenaline suffused her and she could feel it coursing through Nick, too. A mind meld? She didn't know, but she damn sure hoped so. It was time she got some of her stuffing back.

She turned her head as far as possible, to see if they were being followed. Damn it, her eyes wouldn't focus. She blinked and widened them, hoping that would help.

A vehicle sped several car lengths back, an arm with a gun leveled out the passenger window. "Alley, left!" she cried.

A bullet whizzed past her head and she almost lost her grip on him as the bike swerved. He'd nearly laid it on its side.

He had to slow down or risk a pileup. But no, he wasn't only slowing. He was stopping!

"Nick! Keep going! They're right behind us!"

Then she looked around him and saw the problem in duplicate. *Dead end.*

Nick cursed like he never had before. He reached back and gave Cate a shove. "Get off. Behind that Dumpster, quick!" He jumped off the bike, dropped it and rushed for cover, pulling her to relative safety behind him.

"Clip?" she huffed, her breathing jerky as she patted down his pockets.

He felt her hand slip inside his jacket, then heard the clicks as she reloaded. "The alley's so narrow, they're having trouble getting the doors open. One's almost out of the car. Give me the gun, Cate."

"No, I'll do it," she argued, trying to scoot around him.

He shoved her back, snatching the weapon from her hand as he did. The driver, still in the car, was already aiming.

Nick pointed the gun at the windshield, figuring at that range, he could hardly miss. He pulled the trigger and held it, spraying fire across the width of the alley at windshield level. The gun bucked repeatedly, the reports deafening him.

Suddenly it fell silent. His hand felt numb, glued to the weapon as if the metal had melted into his skin. Nerves tingled up his arm to his shoulder. His heart raced, its beat the only thing he could hear.

Cate's hands closed around his and took the gun from him, tugging a bit until he managed to release it. She rested her forehead against his upper arm for a second, then brushed past him. She was walking like a drunk.

Shock, he thought. *He* was experiencing shock. With a huff of anger at himself, he shook it off. He'd seen plenty of death in his career, but this was the first time he had directly caused it. He wondered if Cate had ever…

She was already climbing over the hood, the open door and the dead shooter who had managed to get halfway out of the car. "Find his weapon," she ordered.

Nick obediently crouched and retrieved it from underneath the car's door. Cate was inside the vehicle, her body contorted as she rifled through the driver's pockets. Nick watched through the cracked windshield as she retrieved the dead man's wallet and pistol. She backed out, almost embracing the other body as she searched it, too.

Bloody and tousled, she emerged, climbing over the door onto the hood of the vehicle. "Come on," she said, beckoning to him. "Right over the top. We have to get out of here *now!*"

"What about the police?" he asked, his foot already on the bumper as he climbed. They crawled over the hood and slid off the boot of the car.

She tucked the pistol under one arm and shoved the wallets into his jacket pocket. "I'll call Mercier. He'll straighten it out. For now, I think we'd better find us a ride and get the hell out of Dodge before a posse shows up."

Nick didn't argue. No doubt it was illegal to leave the scene, but his first concern was getting Cate somewhere safe in case there were others out there looking for her.

She peeped out of the alley, then turned to him. "This double vision is hell. What do you think?"

He leaned past her and glanced left, then right. "Looks clear to me. No people around."

"Let's go." Before he could urge caution, she was hurrying down the street, sort of listing to the left as she walked, the pistol she held now tucked into the back of her pants. She was squinting in parked car windows as they went. Suddenly, she stopped, opened the door of a faded green Citroen and crawled half-inside, doing something beneath the steering wheel.

"You're not hotwiring that thing!"

Her mumbled reply sounded affirmative.

"You can't just…steal a car, Cate!"

She grinned up at him. "Honey, I could do it in the dark."

Suddenly as that she had it running, then got out and gestured to him. "But I guess you'd better drive."

Nick knew if he didn't do as she suggested, she'd drive the thing herself. He got in and waited for her to stumble around to the passenger's side.

They sped away. Someone had surely heard shots and reported it. He fully expected to hear the singsong of a siren any second. And no matter what Cate said, he wasn't about to initiate a high-speed chase if that happened.

He drove in silence, relaxing a little after five minutes passed without incident. They were nearing the edge of the city. He turned on the road leading west.

Cate was on her phone reporting to Mercier. Nick tuned out her end of the conversation and concentrated on the road and the rearview mirror, not yet ready to relive the past hour.

"You all right, Nicky?" she asked, her voice gentle. He could feel her assessing gaze on him, but he kept his eyes on the road.

"Are you kidding?" He sped up and shifted, moving with the traffic, concentrating on his driving.

She sighed. "I'm sorry you had to do that."

Nick cleared his throat, uncertain what to say. "Could we not talk about it right now?"

"You'll have to eventually. Even trained agents who have to kill are required to go to counseling after. It's a nuisance, but it does help, no question."

Nick said nothing. What was there to say? He had taken lives today for the first—and he hoped the last—time. Right now, he was pretty revved up and the anger was still ruling. Later, he suspected the impact of what he'd done would hit him.

"You're trained to save lives," she said as if reading his mind. He knew she couldn't do that, of course, no matter what she claimed, but it was still disconcerting whenever she repeated a thought he'd just had.

Hell, everything that had happened since she came back into his life had been disconcerting, to say the very least. It made him wonder what sort of life she'd been leading. A constant adrenaline flow was not good for anyone. She had shot someone today, too, he remembered. "How about you, Cate. Did it bother you?"

"Yes, but there was no choice. Well, there was one, but when it's live or die, I'm gonna choose live every time. I couldn't exactly talk him down. These guys were hired killers. They would have shot us, collected their money and gone on to the next job." She hesitated just a beat. "If I'd let myself stop and consider that the man I was aiming at was some mother's little boy, I'd be dead right now. It's best to concentrate on all the lives you might have saved by doing it."

He got that, but it still wasn't something he wanted to dwell on. Not now anyway. "How about otherwise? You feeling all right?"

She laughed, but it sounded wry, almost bitter. "Dandy. Seeing double, shaky as Jell-O and scared spitless. I could do with a good, stiff drink."

"You drink much?" he asked, more to change the topic than to question her sobriety. He knew Cate would never relinquish control enough to establish a drinking problem.

"No, but a little anesthesia sounds pretty good right now."

"You're recuperating from a head injury. Alcohol's not a good idea. By the way, what do we do now?"

He heard her heave a sigh. "You don't have to patronize me, Nick."

He glanced over at her. "What does that mean? I simply asked you what we should do, Cate. If you don't have a plan, just say so."

"I don't have a plan."

Chapter 5

"Fine!" He pounded his fist on the steering wheel. "No plan. Then I guess we just drive until we run out of gas and then steal another car with a full tank. Didn't you ask your supervisor for some directions? After all, there are several dead bodies of people who were trying to kill you littering the streets and alleys of Florence!"

"You, too, and don't you forget that," she answered succinctly. "And no, I didn't ask Mercier for instructions. He simply told me to hole up somewhere until he could get more people in country. What are you so mad about?"

"I'm not mad, just frustrated!"

"And scared?" she asked. That didn't sound like a taunt to him, but more like she wanted company.

"I'd be a fool if I wasn't and so would you. Did he say where to go?"

In his peripheral vision, Nick could see her massaging her temples with her fingertips.

"Could we pull off the road? I think I'm gonna be sick."

He eased out of traffic, turned down a dirt road and parked behind a copse of trees. Quickly, he jumped out of the car and rounded it as she opened her door. "Come here," he said gently as he helped her out. She slid her arms around his waist, lay her head on his shoulder and held him tight.

Nick brushed a hand over her hair, smoothing it, cradling her head in his palm. "Just relax," he whispered. "I'll take care of you, Catie. I know what to do."

To his astonishment, she began to cry. Not soft little sniffles, either. She cried like a child, gasping, gulping sobs that shook her entire body. For several long moments, he simply held her close, the only thought in his mind to protect and soothe her.

Then, just as suddenly, she recovered and raised her head to look at him. "Sorry about the meltdown." She wiped her face with her sleeve, sniffed and shook her head. "I *never* cry. Everything just seems…too close to the surface since the injury."

"You shouldn't worry about it, Cate. That's to be expected." He smiled down at her. "Still feel nauseous?"

She shook her head and glanced back at the car. "I guess we should go."

"Not yet. No one is after us. I was watching the rearview like a hawk. No one could know where we are. Let's sit here on the grass and unwind for a minute."

She sat down right where she was, legs crossed, and began toying with a dried blade of grass. Nick dropped next to her and took one of her hands in his. Her gaze flew to meet his and he read a question in them that had nothing to do with being chased by gunmen. Were things changing between them?

It was still there, he realized, the feeling she'd had for him when she was just a kid. She didn't even try to conceal it now as she had when they'd met incidentally during the intervening years. Maybe her emotions *were* entirely too close to the surface as she had said. Her guard hadn't just lowered, it seemed to have disappeared, and her vulnerability scared him a little. Cate had always, even as a child, been without doubts, supremely self-confident and in charge of just about everything around her.

"You have an idea where we should go?" she prompted, her voice a bit gruff.

"Sure. I know a place. It's where I intended to take you before…all the excitement."

He drew in a deep breath and looked away from her, trying to absorb the peace of the beautiful Tuscan landscape. Yet his mind's eye was filled with sudden possibilities, a romantic interlude with her in a hidden villa, long walks through gently rolling vineyards where they could steal kisses and taste the warm sun of discovery.

Damn, where had this streak of romanticism come from? This rush of suppressed desire? They were so wrong for each other and they both knew it, had known it and admitted it, agreed on it.

"So where are we going?" she asked, and Nick felt she wasn't really inquiring about any physical destination.

He cleared his throat and released her hand, then leaned back on his elbows, looking at the sky. "If they found us at my apartment, they might be able to trace us if we check into a hotel somewhere. We'd have to use my credit cards. My great-aunt has a small farm about forty miles from here. We'll stay with her."

"We can't involve her in this, Nick," Cate argued. "They know I'm with you. It stands to reason her place would be the next they'd go to."

Nick glanced off in the distance. "No records exist that we're related. My family emigrated before World War II. Hers remained here. When her folks died, she had nothing left. After the war, she changed her name and went into the theater. So there's nothing to connect us. I would never have found her if my grandfather hadn't told me the story when I was little and made me curious. It took months of digging before I located her."

Cate smiled. "Never could resist a puzzle, could you?"

"Nope. This one was worth it, though."

"What did your parents think when you told them you'd found her?"

Nick grinned. "They don't know about Sophia. She and I agreed we would call and surprise them before they left England. Maybe have them fly here to meet her before they return to the States."

"I still think going to her would be risky."

"Not if we weren't followed," Nick argued. "And we weren't, I'm sure of it. Everyone who was after you today is dead. Even if anyone else is interested, it will take them time to get someone in place and we'll have disappeared. You call your people back and let them set up some sort of sting somewhere else to trap whoever is after you. Good plan?"

She laughed. "As a spy, you make a pretty good doctor. What do you know about setting up stings?"

"I used to watch a lot of television," he admitted.

"Okay, let's go meet this auntie of yours and see if she's willing to take in two Yanks on the run."

He stood, gave Cate a hand and pulled her to her feet, resisting the urge to take her in his arms again. She would have come willingly, he knew, but there was no point starting something they couldn't finish. Instead, he held her arm and led her to the car.

Regret washed over him in waves. If only they could somehow reconcile their differences, meet in the middle somewhere. But Cate was Cate and he was who he was, polar opposites, a born adventurer and a pedantic physician, a combination doomed to heartbreak if they pushed their luck and hooked up. He would never be satisfied with a quick fling and Cate would never be in the market for anything long-term. With a dejected sigh, he knew he had to accept how things were.

They rode in silence again, Cate napping, Nick keeping a close check on the road behind them for anyone who might be following. He felt certain no one could be. The car was stolen and no one had seen them take it. If there were any thugs left to give chase, there would have been a confrontation when he and Cate had stopped to rest.

She woke up and stretched.

"There, see it on the hill?" Nick asked, excited about the prospect of seeing Sophia again and introducing her to Cate.

"Make a great postcard or travel ad, wouldn't it?" She sat forward and squinted.

"How's the vision, really?" Nick asked.

"Not so good," she admitted. "It's a little better than it was this morning. I'm sure it'll clear up in time."

Now was not the time for a lecture on acceptance. Nick just prayed he was wrong, that her brain would adjust and compensate. Stranger things had happened with regard to injuries like hers. Still, he didn't hold much hope for that after seeing the hospital's test results.

He drove up the dirt road through the vineyards and parked at the back of the house beneath the trees. Sophia appeared in the doorway of the kitchen before they could get out of the car and waited patiently for them to approach.

She hadn't changed since he had seen her last month. Her silver hair shone, softly waved in a flattering style that concealed her hearing aid. Her makeup was perfectly applied. On her thin frame, she wore a soft lavender blouse belted over dark purple slacks. Her shoes looked sensible, but very expensive.

Ageless and beautiful even at eighty, Nick could imagine the heads Sophia had turned in her prime. Three husbands had left her well fixed financially and she obviously enjoyed life to the max here in her small villa.

"Hello, Aunt Sophia! I've brought a guest, do you mind?"

"Darling boy, you must bring anyone you like to meet me. I am an old woman with few pleasures and your visits are a joy to me." She embraced him with enthusiasm and kissed both sides of his face. "My Nicholas."

"This is Cate Olin. Cate, Sophia Langusta, my great-aunt."

Sophia reached for Cate, grasping her upper arms as she looked her over. "A fine match. You will make strong, beautiful children." She kissed Cate, as well. "Welcome to my home and to our family."

"Wait, ma'am, you're jumping the gun a little. Nick and I grew up together, that's all. Our parents are good friends. But we're not—"

Sophia had already stepped back inside and was beckoning them to join her. "Ahh, it is good! Families are so important. I missed having that for most of my life."

She fluttered her pink polished nails as she gestured to the heavy chairs surrounding the large farm table. "Sit, please! This is a lovely vintage." She handed Nick a bottle of wine and turned to fetch glasses. "We will toast your arrival and your happy future!"

Nick heaved a sigh as he smiled at Cate. When Sophia sat down, he filled her glass, then half filled Cate's.

"Ah, so *that's* the way of things," Sophia said as she nodded knowingly and grinned. She grasped Cate's hand and leaned forward as if to impart a secret. "A bit of wine now and again will not harm the child no matter what they tell you these days."

Cate's eyes flew wide. "No! Oh, no, ma'am, I'm not pregnant!"

Nick laughed. "Cate had a head injury and is on medication, Aunt Sophia, so she can only have a taste of the vino."

"Juice, then," Sophia declared, hopping up again and opening a waist-high refrigerator. "I have grape juice." His aunt moved with surprising agility.

"Please sit with us, Aunt Sophia. I need to explain why we've come."

She returned with a bottle of juice and set it on the table between them. "You have a special reason for the visit?"

Nick nodded. "Someone tried to kill Cate. There was shooting and a car chase in Florence and we barely escaped. However, no one should be able to guess we've come here. Is it all right if we stay for a few days?"

Cate was obviously astounded that he would blurt out the facts that way to an eighty-year-old woman. But Sophia had no doubt faced much worse in her lifetime, having lived in the midst of war. She deserved the truth.

Though she appeared gravely concerned, she certainly didn't seem shocked. "Of course, you must stay! Where else would you go but to family at a time such as this? These people who wish to harm you, they are of this country?"

"We don't know, Ms. Langusta," Cate admitted.

"Do call me Aunt Sophia, dear." She shrugged and took a sip of wine. "Well, whether or not they are, they will not be able to surprise you here. It is a small community and everyone knows everyone else. We would be alerted immediately to strangers arriving and I assure you, we would greet them well armed!"

"Armed?" Cate asked with a short laugh. "You have a weapon?"

Sophia smiled. "My last husband, Guido, had quite a collection and I have not been able to part with so much as a crossbow."

Cate shot Nick a look and repeated, "Crossbow?"

It was true there were several of those, but Sophia also possessed a number of remarkable firearms the local government was not aware existed. In fact, Uncle Guido could have started his own army.

"So, what is being done about these people who threaten your Cate?" Sophia demanded.

"The investigation's ongoing in several countries," Nick assured her. He patiently detailed all that had happened in Switzerland and in Florence. "All we need do here is keep Cate safe while the authorities work it out and make the arrests."

"Pah!" Sophia grimaced and flapped her hand in dismissal of that. "And you trust them to do so? What a sheltered existence you have led, my boy. If there is anything I have learned in life, it is that you must face these matters and handle them yourself!" She raised her fist and waved it for emphasis.

"Nick did shoot two of them," Cate declared in his defense. She bit her lip when he frowned at her, then she added, "And I shot one. They had killed at least one of the agents who were designated to protect us, probably both."

Sophia's eyebrows raised as she regarded Nick in a new light. "Well done!"

Nick felt the welling of guilt in his gut. So far he hadn't

had time to reflect much on his taking lives, but now it hit him full force. Still, they had left him no choice. If he hadn't done what he had, he and Cate would be dead in that alley.

It worried him a bit that Cate seemed to feel no remorse at all. Her actions had been so automatic, she'd performed perfectly in spite of her new limitations. She couldn't see straight enough to drive a car, but from the back of a moving motorcycle, she'd dropped a man in his tracks. Instinct and intensive training, he supposed.

She must do this on a regular basis. He was sorry for the incident that had ended her career, but thanked God those days were over for her. Or almost over. First, they had to eliminate the current problem. Then she would have to find another occupation.

"Come, if you are finished, I will show you to your room," Sophia said as she got up from the table.

"Rooms," Nick clarified. "We will need two, Aunt Sophia."

"Of course you will," she said with a tinkling laugh.

"Matchmaker!" Nick mouthed to Cate behind Sophia's back.

"Charming." Cate whispered. She smiled and took his arm as they climbed the stairs.

They settled in their respective rooms, temptingly adjacent, Cate noted. Sophia was probably not well-known for subtlety. Her whole attitude made Cate smile. That was one feisty lady. She reminded Cate of her teammates. Rather, her *former* teammates. Cate's smile faded like a cheap T-shirt.

Her head ached almost as much as her heart. What would she do if she couldn't do what she did best? How would she ever reconcile herself to the boredom?

At the moment, she couldn't deal with that possibility. She crawled onto the high tester bed and was asleep in moments. When she awoke, Nick was sitting in the chair beside the window, reading.

"You don't have to watch me every minute," she grumbled. "It's embarrassing, you watching me sleep. What if I drool or something?"

He flipped a page and glanced up. "I'd wipe your chin. It's what I do." He returned his attention to the book.

Cate rolled over and tried to sleep again, but couldn't with him in the room. "Why are you in here?"

"Aunt Sophia is having my room aired. She suggested it."

"Ha!"

"My reaction precisely," Nick admitted with a smile, "but she insisted. She thinks we make a lovely couple."

"Ha!" Cate repeated.

"Humor her. She's old and has few pleasures."

"Yeah, so she said, but I don't believe that for a hot second. Look at this place! She's living in the lap of luxury, probably has a lover down the road, all the wine she can drink, and she's obviously richer than God."

Nick laughed and closed the book. "Yes, but she loves having family around her. She's been busy online ordering us clothes and shoes like we are her newly adopted orphans, which I suppose we are. She's been a little lonely, I think."

Cate rolled onto her back and stared up at the canopy

above her. "Enter the poor, beleaguered nephew, her only visiting relative. Prospective heir to the Tuscan estate, perhaps?"

"Never thought of that and I doubt she has," Nick said conversationally. "I expect she has other plans in place."

"I was only teasing you, Nick. You love her, don't you?"

"I do," Nick admitted. "She's great, isn't she?"

"Totally. It makes me nervous, though, staying here. I wouldn't want her in danger."

"Neither would I. If I thought there was the slightest chance we were followed, I wouldn't have come. Even your boss doesn't know where we are," he reminded her.

"Oh, yes," Cate informed him. "Mercier knows where I am at all times."

"You told him? What if there's a mole in your organization or something?" Nick demanded. He got up and stood beside the bed, accusing. "How could you?"

"Didn't. I have an implant, a tracker."

"A microchip thing?"

"Larger, about quarter size. Better range." She tapped the top of her shoulder. "We all have them so we can be located even when *we* don't know where we are."

"Like if you're kidnapped?"

She nodded. "Or captured."

"Or killed," he added in a whisper.

"We haven't lost an agent yet." She smiled. "There are no moles on our team, Nick. You watch entirely too much television."

He gazed out the window, his expression worried. "They found you in Florence."

Chapter 6

Nick borrowed Sophia's computer and accessed Cate's records at the hospital in Valais. He searched for an explanation for her sudden burst of agility and coordination during their escape from Florence. Given her injury, she shouldn't have been able to perform at that level. He realized, of course, that adrenaline must account for most of it. Grit and determination plus survival instincts had kicked in, as well. Amazing effect. But then, Cate had always amazed him.

He sat back in the chair, tapping his chin with his fingers as he studied the results of her last CT scan and MRI. Could she somehow recover completely? And what did it say about him as a doctor, as a person who cared about her, that he didn't really want her to?

Her prognosis for full recovery was highly improbable according to her doctors. He had convinced himself they were right and tried to convince her, as well. But of course they would have given the worst-case scenario rather than provide her with false hope. And they didn't know Cate the way he did.

She was exhausted after the ordeal and was sleeping almost constantly their second day at the villa. He woke her periodically to eat, drink and take her meds, which he had stuffed in the small duffel they'd brought with them.

"Hey! What are you up to?" she asked from the doorway of Sophia's study. Her shoulder braced against the door frame, she appeared steady on her feet.

Nick quickly logged off. "Surfing, catching up on the news. How are you feeling?"

"Rested. Only a little goofy." She grinned. "But I managed to stay upright for the last quarter hour and I only see one of you. Good, huh?"

"Excellent," he replied honestly. "Let's not overdo it, though. A quarter hour is probably enough exercise, especially after all you went through during our great escape."

She scoffed. "Don't make an invalid of me, Nick. I have to get over this and lying around like this won't do it."

He got up and approached her, smoothing her hair back behind her ears. "Neither will behaving like Superwoman. Baby steps are better at the beginning."

She placed a palm on his chest and looked up at him. "What do I do to get my sea legs back?"

Nick sighed. "Give your brain time to make new connections." Maybe he should warn her again that it might never do that, but his conscience warred with his need to keep her safe, dependent. "Time is the key."

She pushed back out of his reach, listed to one side and quickly propped her hand against the wall to steady herself. "Hell with that. I have to get back up to speed. I *know* I can do it. I've already discovered a few tricks that help some."

"Excuse me!" Sophia appeared, somewhat out of breath. Her face was white as chalk. "There's a man at the door who insists he knows Cate. He says it's important he speak to her. His name is Vinland."

Nick's heart nearly stopped. Then he remembered Cate's revelation about the tracker she wore. If someone were here to kill her, they would hardly knock and announce themselves. Even so, he retrieved the weapon he kept nearby just in case.

"You can put that away," Cate said. "Jack sent him."

"Why would Mercier send someone when they could be followed? I don't like this, Cate."

But she was already halfway out of the room. Nick hurried to catch up and put his arm around her, the gun still in his hand.

Vinland wasn't waiting at the front door. He met them in the foyer. "Hey, Cate! Well, don't you look…different! Hair's, well, *interesting*."

"Thanks. Ever-changing, that's me! What's up?"

"I'm coming off a case in Sand Land. Since it's a sure thing I'm off everyone's radar right now, Jack said stop by and see how you are and if you need anything. Heard you shot up good ol' Firenze yesterday and left a real mess."

"Heisted a car, too," Cate announced proudly. "Jack fix that for me?"

"Paid for. Seller's happy. The Florence cops aren't too thrilled, but they'll get over it. Your targets were hired help, as I'm sure you've guessed. An assassin team, of all things. Family business. You pretty much wiped them out."

Nick interrupted. "Could we take this back into the library there so Cate can sit? She's been up too long as it is."

Vinland raised an eyebrow. "You're real persuasive waving that piece around. Dr. Sandro, I presume?" He held out his hand. "Eric Vinland."

Nick had his hands full, one on Cate and the other holding the weapon. He merely looked at Vinland's hand, then back at the face of the man who regarded him with no little amusement. Cocky bastard. Too good-looking. Blond like Cate, tanned as a beach bum, tall and fit. He wondered just how well Cate knew this guy. He was shooting her some knowing glances Nick didn't like at all. "You sure you weren't tailed?"

Vinland laughed. "Positive." He led the way into Sophia's library and waited until Cate was seated in one of the leather chairs beside the fireplace.

Nick looked down at the gun he was holding, wondering if it was safe to put it away.

Vinland didn't flinch. "Yeah, you can put that away for now, Doc. If I were a danger to her, you would never have known I was here and Cate would already be dead."

Cate reached for Nick's gun. "Give me that before it goes off. Eric's here to help."

Nick held the pistol out of reach. He still wasn't certain

the man could be trusted. Besides, he didn't like the famil-
iarity with which this Vinland guy looked at Cate, as if they
shared some secret. He just didn't look serious enough to suit
Nick.

"Okay, then," Vinland said with a sigh and proceeded
to ignore Nick and the gun. "Cate, the woman you tailed
through Canada and took down in Seattle two months ago
was the sister of Ahmed Adin, a rich rogue from Saudi."

Nick interrupted. "You killed her?"

Vinland leaped to Cate's defense. "She was wired from
neck to navel, a briefcase with a dirty bomb in one hand
and a detonator in the other. Cate had no time for another
solution. There is only one spot in the human body where
a bullet will drop a perp and kill any reflex." He pointed
to his neck. "Cate made that remarkable shot and saved a
helluva lot of lives."

"I would never judge Cate," Nick told him. "I only
asked."

Cate threw up her hands. "Knock off the testosterone
party, guys. Now what's the plan, Eric?"

Vinland straightened his collar and nodded. "I've been
shadowing Adin ever since that happened to see if he had
plans to send someone in her place to complete her little
jihad," Vinland said. "She was dying of cancer and you
screwed her plans to cover herself in glory and Yankee
blood. Win all those male virgins in paradise." He wiggled
his eyebrows suggestively.

"I don't think that goes for the females," Cate said.

"Well, maybe she was going for it just in case and you
interrupted her. Her brother's bound to be mighty mad

about that. Not the male virgins, just her place in nirvana."
He shot Nick a dark look as he spoke to Cate. "Good
work, by the way. Heard you got a medal."

"Everybody else heard about it, too, unfortunately."
Cate inclined her head and clicked her tongue. "So this
Adin's a real believer, huh? I'd rather deal with some
greedy jerk after power any day than a devout jihadist out
for revenge. Are we sure he's behind this?"

"He looks good for it, but Jack and the others are ex-
hausting every other possibility, going over all your past
cases with COMPASS and before that, too. He wants you
to stay here and only call in if you think of anyone else
who might want you dead. Adin's on the move, but I'll find
him. Last word, he was in Germany, so I'll start there. If
he's gone home, I'll fly back to Saudi and get him."

"Sounds like a suicide mission," Nick commented.

Cate laughed. "A walk in the park for Eric. He's culti-
vated quite a name for himself in the Middle East. Best
undercover we've got. Master of disguise, speaks fluent
Arabic and several other languages."

Vinland put his hands together and bowed. "You are too
kind." Then he did get serious. "It's time to disappear,
Cate. For good."

"The hell you say," she replied. "Let's just eliminate the
problem and be done with it. Go get rid of him."

"The tentacles won't stop working if we cut off the
head. The man's got international ties and oil money to
back them up. Those goons in Florence and the shooter in
Switzerland, for instance, were local hitters, infidels he
probably paid top dollar."

"*If* he's the one who hired them," Cate added.

Vinland shrugged. "Yeah, but even if he's not, some-body's contract is out on you, Cate. I can't neutralize every hit man on the planet." He sighed and shrugged. "I think our best bet is to announce the contract's been fulfilled, provide some bogus proof of it, make you vanish and give you a new identity outside the business."

"Damn it, *no!*" She turned away and crossed her arms over her chest. "I'm not ready to quit. Change my looks, give me a new name, put me on another team and I can still work."

"Aside from your diminished capabilities, if you resur-face in any intel capacity, even in admin somewhere, you'd be made in a minute. The word would be out." He smiled ruefully. "Your looks are not exactly unremarkable. We could change your hair and face, but unless you shrink a foot in height and alter the way you move, there's no way to hide you."

"The way I move's already been altered," she grumbled.

Vinland shared a pleading look with Nick. He obvi-ously needed help in convincing her, but Nick was out of arguments. Vinland tried again. "Face it, Cate, you were outed in the news. Jack might have been able to use you on backup details, but running your own ops was already a thing of the past. Now your reflexes are not what they were due to your injury. The director would put you in a basement somewhere analyzing data just to keep you out of sight. You'd be happier plowing corn in Iowa."

Cate shook her head. "No."

Nick felt obligated to give it another shot. Vinland had

come here to help. "It's really not your call, Catie. Why not do as he suggests? It makes good sense."

She turned on him, fuming and visibly shaking. "Sense? Are you kidding? You just want me out of it, don't you! Well, I'd be out of it all right if they relocate me! Out of not only *your* life, but that of my parents and all my friends. It's exactly like the Witness Security Program. Everyone and everything I know, I'd have to give up totally. No further contact ever!"

Nick was appalled. "But surely you could—"

Again she shook her head. "And then I'd have to come up with something else I could do that didn't involve anything remotely connected to intel or any other sort of law enforcement."

She slammed her fisted hands to her chest. "This is who I am, don't you get that?" Her frantic gaze jerked to Vinland to include him in the question. Tears streamed down her cheeks. Without another word, she ran from the room, off balance, staggering as if she could hardly see.

Nick started after her but Vinland grasped his arm. "Wait. Let her go. She just needs a little time to work it out for herself. She knows we're right."

"Work out *what*?" Nick demanded. "She's not going to do this! She can't just…leave *everything!*"

Vinland sighed and released him, but stood in his way. "Can't leave *you*, Doc, isn't that what changed your mind? Wouldn't you give her up to save her life?"

Nick bowed his head and clenched his eyes. "Of course I would. I'd die for her if I could."

"Then do it! I'll kill you off, too," Vinland suggested.

"Take her somewhere and the both of you start over. We'll help you create new identities, start new careers. I understand yours is pretty much in the toilet anyway." He glanced at Nick's right hand.

Nick shot him a hateful look. "Not much for tact, are you?"

Vinland shrugged. "Waste of time. If you love Cate, you'll do it."

"Love her?" Nick said with a laugh. "What the hell gave you that idea?"

The agent's eyebrows rose and a smile played around his lips. "*Die for her,* you said? That right there gave me a hefty clue, doc."

"I knew her as a kid. I care about her. A lot. I owe her family."

"Yeah, right. Well, okay. If you *care,* convince her. I'll get ol' Ahmed soon as I can find him and get around his security, but there's no way to know who'll pop up to replace him and whether they'll honor his obsession to avenge his sister. They tend to have big families and his is no exception."

"You seem pretty sure it's him."

"Yeah, but we're still hedging all bets." He glanced out the doorway where Cate had exited. "Okay, go do your stuff now and make her see the light. I've got to run, but I'll be in touch. You should be safe here for the time being."

"Wait." Nick frowned at him. "Find another way for her, Vinland." He hesitated only a second and added, "Please."

"I don't think there is one or we'd be doing it. We'll miss her, too. She was one of the best in the business."

Without another word, Vinland left. Nick sat down and covered his face with his hands. God, what a mess. His problems from a couple of weeks ago seemed minute compared to today's.

"She can do it," Sophia said softly, her fingers pressing his shoulder. "You both can. You should."

They had totally forgotten about her, but she had heard everything. Nick shouldn't be glad of that, but he was. The comfort of a loving touch meant a lot at the moment. "You don't understand what it would mean for her, Aunt Sophia. A total reinvention."

Her soft, bitter laugh reminded him of her background.

"Sorry, I forgot. I guess you do know," he amended and reached to pat the hand on his shoulder. "I guess you do."

He wondered if Cate would look back on this someday in the distant future with as many regrets as Sophia suffered. Loss of family, friends, career, everything familiar.

That must be a lot like death of sorts. But her real death was not going to be an option. He had already discovered he would do anything to keep Cate alive, even kill without hesitation.

He had a bad feeling this wasn't going to be quite as easily resolved as Vinland suggested.

Cate dried her eyes and cursed her weakness. How the devil could she have let Eric see her vulnerability? He'd surely report it and that would verify Jack's decision. Even if she hadn't said a word or shown any response at all, Eric would have picked up on it. He was a damn good telepath.

She had felt him probing her mind with his. He *knew*, damn it. She didn't need her psychic ability to know that he knew she no longer had hers. Deliberately, she had opened her mind and thought the words, knowing he would read her. *You lost it once, too, but you got it back, damn you!* Couldn't Eric remember what it was like? He had temporarily lost his ability to read people at a critical juncture in one of his cases. His break had been purely psychological, not due to trauma like hers, but he'd still lost it and Mercier hadn't forcibly retired *him*.

"Oh God, I've lost everything!" she groaned, hating her reaction to that almost as much as the fact itself. Where had her strength gone? Her backbone? Angrily, she dashed away the tears that streaked down her face.

Hadn't she performed okay back in Florence despite the problem with her sight and equilibrium? Those would return to normal with time. She knew it. But this horrible tendency to display her emotions had to clear up sooner than that or she'd screw any chance she had of keeping her job. If she had any chance left. Or if she even lived through this.

"I'd rather die," she muttered to herself.

"No!" Nick rushed into her bedroom and threw his arms around her as if she were already holding a gun to her head.

She pushed against his chest, leaned back and looked up at him. "I didn't mean it that way! I meant I'd rather die *trying!*"

He kissed her. His mouth came down on hers, catching it open. His tongue invaded and he virtually inhaled her.

His arms crushed her to him, hands grasping almost desperately at her back, her waist, her hips.

Cate gave as good as she got, meeting him with a pent-up passion that sent shock waves through her body like a taser. Only not painful, she realized as she plundered that long forbidden pleasure she'd dreamed of for so long. No pain at all. Pure unadulterated pleasure.

His body hard against hers, she leaned toward the bed. The move seemed to pull him from whatever spell had enveloped them both. His mouth left hers as suddenly as it had descended. He steadied her with his hands on her shoulders, his fingers pressing deeply. "I'm so sorry, Cate," he whispered.

She smiled and drew in a deep breath, releasing it in a huff. "I'm not."

"Not about the kiss," he declared.

"Thank goodness for that," she murmured, feeling giddy all over. All she could think was that he didn't regret kissing her, that he'd been as overcome as she was. Maybe more and certainly first. That he'd probably do it again with very little encouragement. Every nerve in her body sang with anticipation.

He walked her over to the bed. "Sit down. We have to talk."

"Enough talk," she told him, offering him a slumberous look.

"Now's not the time. We have to make some plans." But he did take a seat beside her and held one of her hands in both of his.

She looked down at his long, capable fingers with their

short blunt nails. Lifesaving hands. Hands that had delved into the mysteries of the brain, solving those one by one with his God-given talent. Hands she had caused to take lives. She brought them to her lips and realized her face was wet again with tears. *Damn it!*

"Help me get over this, Nick," she whispered angrily. "You have to. Something's haywire, making me not myself. I *never* cry!"

"Post-traumatic stress," he assured her, but she could see he was holding something back.

"And?" she prompted.

He squeezed her hand. "Cate, it's hard to determine just how much of your change in personality is physical and how much is emotional, due to all that's happened to you. Time, therapy and observation are the only tools we have to determine that."

"And precious little time," she said with an inelegant snort. "I'll either give up the therapy and observation or be killed if I stick around to take advantage of it." She shoved his hands away and stood, embracing herself. "In any event, I'm not likely to be normal again. Ever."

His silence frightened her more than anything had.

She turned and demanded the truth. "Am I?"

"We all change constantly, Cate. Some changes are rapid, unfortunate and forced on us. We deal with those the best we can and get on with our lives."

"Ha! That's easy for you to say. Nobody scrambled *your* brains!"

"No, that's true," he admitted. Then he held up his right hand so she could see. "However, somebody took a knife to my hand and ended my existence as a surgeon. You're not the only one making things up as you go. But I'm further along with it than you are and maybe I could give you a few pointers on how to deal with it. All right, Catie?"

Her heart nearly stopped. Wide-eyed, she examined his hand. She had noticed the pink scar on his right palm, but hadn't asked him about it. How could she have been so self-absorbed?

Why hadn't he told her before? Because he was exaggerating, fitting his experience to hers in order to gain her cooperation in therapy, maybe?

"You'll operate again," she insisted, "Soon as that heals, you'll do exercises, get treatments or surgery. Your hand does work, Nick! I've seen it work!" Felt it, too, she remembered, holding her, squeezing the muscles of her back.

Cutting her hair. Squeezing a trigger...oh, wait, he was a lefty. She stared at the scar. It was still pink, but obviously healed already.

He flexed his fingers. "Yeah, it works to some extent. It's been nearly a year. Fine motor skills are definitely gone, though. Lost the touch it takes to do what I did. But that's okay, Cate. I'm all right with it and you'll be okay, too, eventually. At least you aren't paralyzed or severely incapacitated. There are plenty of things you'll be able to do and do well."

She was already shaking her head. "Damn it, my work is my life!"

"Then you'll make a new life, Catie," he told her. His voice was persuasive now, cajoling, enticing as hell. For a long second, their eyes held. She waited for him to add, "With me." But he didn't say it.

For a second, just from the look on his face, his tone, and the memory of his kiss, she was tempted to say a vehement yes anyway and fall into his arms. But no. He wanted her and they both knew it, but they also knew what was holding him back.

Even considering that she might not recover fully and be able to resume her former activities, she had made too many enemies already. She was a danger magnet and Nick needed peace and harmony in his life. No matter what she did with herself, she could never bring him that.

His only real foes were death and disablement, which he had fought valiantly in operating rooms. He would continue to fight on some medical front, no doubt. She had already dragged him too far away from his familiar battleground.

Reluctantly she looked away. "I can't be what I'm not. I'm a well-trained agent, Nick. It's what I do. It's what I *am.*"

He pushed up from the bed and stormed out of the room, muttering, "Stubborn, bullheaded adrenaline junkie!"

Guilty. Cate sighed and flopped back down on the bed. "Don't be kind, Nicky," she shouted after him. "Say what you really think."

Things hadn't changed a bit. They had fought this same fight as kids and would forever if they didn't go separate ways again.

It hurt that he saw her the way he did, but she certainly couldn't deny it any more than she could change it.

Chapter 7

Nick felt the weight of Cate's anxiety and spent the next two days watching her exhaust herself.

Sophia had provided them with clothes, shoes and even makeup for Cate. His aunt seemed to have thought of everything, except how to persuade her female guest to accept the downtime and relax. Nick wondered if there was any way anyone could do that.

Other than strengthening her muscles, he could see no progress in spite of Cate's efforts, probably *because* of those efforts. She was overdoing it and he couldn't convince her to slow down.

The plans she was making worried him, too, not only due to what they were, but because she had concocted them on impulse and begun to set them in motion. Nothing swayed her. If she couldn't go back to work for the COMPASS team, then she would start a private company of her own.

She was already making calls, arranging for office space in McLean, Virginia, checking on her savings and retirement funds to see how many employees she could afford to hire. The very thought scared the life out of Nick. She'd be a sitting duck for every assassin out there if she didn't take Vinland's advice, fake her death and set up a new identity.

Today they were walking through vineyards now bereft of leaves, a rather desolate landscape in winter. Nick felt a little desolate himself. "Cate, I wish you'd put off all this business, at least until the investigation's complete."

She stopped walking, smiled and raised her face to the stiff, cold breeze. "You think I'm moving too fast. I get that, but it is my decision."

Nick tugged the collar of her coat up to cover her neck. "You shouldn't be contacting anyone, given this situation. It's almost as if you *want* to be found and that's danger-ously self-destructive, Cate."

She faced him, squinting from the sun. "I have to *do* something, Nick, not just sit around and hide. Besides, I'm not an idiot. I've been very careful about the inquiries I've made. My phone is totally secure and no one can trace our location from it. You're just mad because I'm taking matters into my own hands and didn't ask your permission first."

"Or anyone's, apparently. I talked to Mercier this morn-ing. He's not happy. He did promise you a job of some kind when you're better."

She made a rude noise and continued walking down the sandy row between the vines. "*Better,* not well. No one expects me to beat this. No one but *me,*" she added.

Nick slid a hand beneath her elbow to steady her as they walked. "You'd improve faster if you didn't rush it so much. I know that seems to make little sense on the surface, but you are overextending your energy, stressing yourself out and slowing your own progress."

At that she halted in her tracks, grabbed his chin between her thumb and forefinger and peered directly into his eyes. "Seriously, Nick? Or are you just trying to hold me back because you think I'm safer here than anywhere else?"

The accusation stung. Maybe it was partially true. He glanced away, then realized his mistake. He should have held her gaze.

"Thought so," she said, pinching his chin hard and walking on, stuffing her hands in her pockets. Her foot caught on a root and she stumbled.

Nick caught her before she fell. "Damn it, Cate! Slow down!"

When he turned her around to head back to the house, he noticed the tears streaming down her cheeks. She didn't say a word and he didn't, either. What more could he say?

She jerked out of his grasp and went on ahead of him. This walk through the vineyards wasn't exactly the romantic stroll he had visualized on the way here. The bleakness of it represented just how skewed his fantasies about Cate really were. Reality sucked.

She walked on, eyes straight ahead, hands in her

pockets for warmth. He noted that she balanced a whole lot better when she was distracted and not worrying about it. Odd. Maybe her abject fear of *not* progressing was actually hampering her progress.

He began to wonder how much of her impairment was psychosomatic and how much was physiological. She would need more tests to determine that. He certainly had a weird mix of feelings about *that* possibility.

They reached the back of the house and entered the kitchen where he helped her take off her coat.

Sophia had hot tea and date cakes waiting for them, but she was absent. He noticed that in addition to throwing them together at every opportunity, she also provided plenty of privacy. His great-aunt seemed to think it was her mission in life to pair them off permanently.

Funny how everybody seemed to think they were a perfect match except for the two parties involved. He wondered if his resistance had been rooted in resentment when he was younger. What else could have made him rebel so steadfastly against the very thing he wanted?

Nick smiled to himself. If he thought he could stand a life of constant exasperation, he might go for it now. If only he could persuade Cate to live some semblance of a normal life. If, if, if...

He would try anything. "When we've finished here, I'm going to Colombia to work with one of the missions there," he announced. "The rebels keep shooting the locals because they'd rather produce coffee than drugs. They need doctors."

She swerved around and stared at him. "You're *what?*"

He inclined his head. "Can't do brain surgery, but I can still practice to some extent, maybe save a few people. At least I won't need malpractice insurance there."

"That's a bald-faced lie!" she almost shouted the words.

"Why do you say that? They'll be too glad to have any kind of medical care to sue me if I screw up."

She frowned, shaking her head in confusion. "That's just…stupid! You know I don't mean the insurance!" She threw up her hands. "The whole thing. You? In South America? In the jungle with rebels?"

Suddenly she stilled and her eyebrows drew together. "Oh, it's a joke, right?"

"You see me laughing?"

"No, but you just made it all up. You have a point to make and that's how you're doing it. Scare me. Show me how it feels to be scared for you!" She rolled her eyes. "Okay, I get it. You're scared for *me*, but that's no reason to lie, Nick."

"Did it work?" he asked, trying to sound reasonable when what he really wanted to do was shake some sense into her.

"Well, the difference is that I *know* what I'm doing and you wouldn't. Not down there working in the jungle, dodging drug lords. What a crock."

"Hey, I could do it. I can shoot," he reminded her. "Proved it, didn't I?"

She rolled her eyes heavenward, "A drunk monkey couldn't have missed at that range! You did okay when forced to it, but face facts, Nicky, you aren't geared for confrontation. At least not that kind."

He granted her that, but he wasn't through. "Like you, I have to do *something* with my life. All I'm saying is that neither of us should latch on to the first alternative that comes to mind.

"We need to think outside our own wants, Cate, and consider where we can do the most good for the most people." He picked up a date cake and placed it on his plate. "And as much as I want to keep performing surgery in any venue possible—in this case, as a volunteer in the wilds—it would be self-serving and not in the interest of any patient who came under my knife. I could cost someone their life. So could you if you go back in the field. So, yes, I lied to make a point. Actually, two points."

Cate sat down, propped her chin on her fists and looked lost in thought. He hoped she was rethinking her plans for the future, but it wasn't likely.

Finally she broke the silence. "So what do you really intend to do?"

Good sign, he thought. She was thinking outside herself, finally, and considering someone else's problems. Since she was interested, he gave her the truth. "Changing specialties, a fellowship in psychiatry at Johns in Baltimore. Starts in three months."

"Psychiatry, huh?" She shifted restlessly in her chair. "Ah, light dawns. That's why they delegated you to babysit me, right? Don't you lie to me again," she warned.

He filled her cup and then his with the steaming aromatic brew Sophia had prepared. "Undoubtedly that's why they *let* me. I do know about brains, yours in particular, and have a pretty good understanding of what you're facing." He held up his right hand. "They thought I could guide you through the change."

Her gaze dropped to the tea in her cup where she stared as if she could read leaves in the bottom. "So, have I truly lost it?"

Nick smiled. "Your mind? No. Your impulse control? Maybe. Your balance is still out of whack. Vision seems about the same. As for your old job, Cate, the answer is yes, you *have* lost that. You will not be a field agent again." He sighed. "I'm sorry, but as you know, Mercier promised he will reassign you if you're able to perform training or something of that nature."

"Whoop-de-do," she grumbled. "Maybe we should both go to Colombia, then." She added a twisted grin. "You could save the good guys while I mow down the bad. I guess I could shoot at least as well as you could operate."

Nick smiled at her lame joke. "So you'll hold off on pursuing that new business of yours? At least for a while?"

She nodded.

He felt sad for her, but also relieved. Maybe she was beginning to accept what fate had dealt her.

Then he noticed she was not looking him in the eye, but glancing off to one side, just as he had done when he had lied to her.

"Catie…" he said with a tone of warning.

She raised her hand to ward him off. "Okay, okay. I won't pursue any new ventures." Still, he sensed a *but* in the reassurance.

"What do you intend to do then? I might as well know since I'm sure you've got something cooking inside that head of yours."

She studied her cup again, tracing the design on it with

her finger. "I need to do some research online. You know, just check on some things that might have to do with the case." She cut her gaze sideways to meet his. "No harm in that, right?"

"Guess not. You have an idea about someone besides Adin who might be behind the shooting? You should tell Mercier. They have more resources to investigate than you do here."

Her nod acknowledged that. "You and Jack want me doing sit-down work. That's what this involves. Safe as knitting."

Nick covered her hand with his and gave it a squeeze. "I'd definitely like to see you doing something safe for a change."

"You got it," she said, turning her hand so that she clasped his palm. This time those guileless blue eyes met his squarely without so much as a second's hesitation.

And it still felt like a lie.

An hour later, after getting her hostess's permission, Cate secluded herself in the library with Sophia's computer. She intended to visit every medical site she could find online that listed symptoms resulting from head injuries and/or oxygen deprivation. When she was satisfied that Nick wasn't trying to hold her back or exaggerate her prognosis, she would get to work on the investigation of the shooting.

Depression threatened to overtake her, as it usually did when she was alone, but she fought it. The only way she knew how to do that was with work. Something productive. Exactly what she told Nick she would do.

She might not have her telepathic powers now, but there was nothing wrong with her memory. The codes for the supposedly secure Web sites set up by known terrorists would provide her with nearly as much info as the team would have.

Eric had given her the name of the man they thought was behind the attempt on her life. She would start there.

"We'll just see how good you are at sedentary investigations," she muttered. But first, she would dig into the medical stuff.

Feeling jittery with expectation, Cate turned on the computer. While it booted, she dragged a small tablet out of the right-hand drawer of the desk and found a ballpoint pen to take notes.

She absently scribbled her name at the top while she waited, then tapped the pen against the paper, making little dots. The singsong of the audio signaled that the computer was ready and she leaned closer to the screen.

Icons appeared, the same as were on her own computer at home. But beneath them were lines of gibberish. She squinted and refocused. Not Italian. Not any language she recognized.

Cate sat back in the chair and took a deep breath. She looked out the window, shook her head, then peered back at the screen. Still the marks meant nothing. Apprehension heightened as she slid her finger across the small touch pad and moved the cursor to one of the symbols she recognized that should open the browser. She tapped it.

The screen blossomed with color and boxes for ads. Breath rushed out of her lungs in a moan.

Panicked, she pushed back from the desk and pressed her palms to her head. "Nicky!" she screamed. "Nicky!"

Nick dropped the book he was reading and snatched up the weapon he always kept nearby. He dashed for the library fully expecting to find an intruder attempting to kill her.

Instead, she sat doubled over in the desk chair, face in her hands, sobbing like a child. After glancing around to make sure no one threatened her, he laid the gun on the desk and knelt on the floor beside her.

Gently, he pried her hands away. "Look at me, Catie. What's wrong? Are you in pain? Where does it hurt?"

She struggled to get her breath and gestured at the computer. What had she found that frightened her so much? He checked the screen. Nothing but the open homepage with the usual stuff. He quickly screened the news headlines there. Nothing appeared that should freak her out. She was clutching his hand, her nails biting his skin. He turned back to her. "What? Tell me."

"I...can't...read it!" she cried.

Nick frowned. This shouldn't be happening. She'd already been tested and he'd seen the results. Her verbal, reading, writing and comprehension skills had been intact. Even her memory hadn't suffered.

He noticed the pad on the desk and peered at the top page. Squiggles and dots. Had she tried to write something? He picked it up. "What's this?" he asked.

She looked at the paper he put in her lap. "My name," she whispered in a jerky little breath. "It's not right."

"That's okay," he said soothingly, brushing the fringe

of her bangs back from her furrowed brow. "It doesn't matter right now."

He rose and pulled her to her feet. "You need to lie down for a bit while I figure this out. It will be okay, Cate. I promise it will be okay. Come on now." He led her out of the library and up the stairs to her room. She moved like an automaton. The sick feeling in his stomach grew worse with each minute that passed.

He helped her lie down, pulled off her shoes and covered her with the soft wool throw from the foot of the bed. She snuggled into it, drawing herself into a fetal position as she closed her eyes.

Nick leaned down and kissed her temple. "Just sleep for a while, sweetheart. It's nothing to worry about. You just need rest."

Oh, hell, how he could lie! He wasn't only worried, he was frantic. With monumental effort, he stood very still, sucked in a deep breath and remembered he was a physician first and always. There were things he must do, answers he needed in order to help Cate. His *patient,* he reminded himself.

So what was he to do without his bag of tools. Vital signs, he reminded himself. He pressed his fingertips at Cate's carotid artery and took her pulse. Fast, but not alarming. His hand moved automatically to her forehead. No fever. He lifted her eyelids and checked her pupils as sunlight from the window caused them to contract. Normal. She had fallen sound asleep too quickly to suit him.

Resumed bleeding in the brain could have caused this. So could an infection resulting from the surgery, though that should have shown up before now. Maybe the activity in Florence had exacerbated the damage she already had. In any case, he needed to get her to a hospital right away.

The problem with that was using her identification to get her registered at one. He could take her in as a Jane Doe, he supposed, but then he couldn't explain about her former treatment in Switzerland.

There was only one thing he could do. He hurried downstairs, spoke briefly with his aunt about his plans, then went to construct a bed for Cate in the backseat of her stolen car. Within half an hour, he had her loaded, still half asleep, and on her way back to Florence.

He took her straight to Nuovo San Giovanni di Dio Hospital. They had the facilities for what he needed, but he had no license to practice in this country. And Cate had no passport, identification or insurance available. He only hoped he could rely on professional courtesy and get things done.

An hour later, he was still butting his head against the wall of the local medical association, personified by the chief of medicine, Dottore Purpura, while Cate languished on a sofa in the doctor's lounge.

He gave up cajoling and went straight to coercion. Punching Mercier's number on his cell, he suffered through two rings before he got an answer. "Cate's worse and needs tests immediately. I'm at Nuovo San Giovanni di Dio Hospital and they refuse to let me use the machines. Do something," he ordered.

At Mercier's command, Nick shoved the phone at Dr. Purpura. "Talk to this man."

Purpura listened for a couple of minutes, his expression

changing from righteous belligerence to confusion to concern. He handed the phone back to Nick. "We will begin with a CT scan," the man announced, "then proceed to the MRI."

"And an EEG," Nick demanded.

Purpura nodded. "I will call for a gurney."

"Never mind," Nick snapped. "I'll bring her myself." He marched over and lifted Cate from the sofa. "Lead on."

He followed the doctor to radiology and the testing began. Nick oversaw every move they made and examined the results with a keen eye. When he found no cause for alarm on any of the tests, he insisted their radiologist and two other doctors double-check his findings and they all agreed.

Cate seemed virtually oblivious to everything and everybody. She responded when ordered directly to do something, but never questioned, protested or seemed the least bit interested. He worried it was the first stage of coma.

"This apathy is directly opposed to her usual involvement," he said, voicing his worry to Purpura, who had become inordinately interested in the new patient. The doctor remained wary of Nick, or at least of Nick's association with the enigmatic Jack Mercier. Cate's old boss must have put the fear of God into him.

"What would you deduct from her lack of reaction?" Nick asked Purpura.

"Perhaps delayed post-traumatic stress?" the doctor suggested.

"Why do you think so?" Nick insisted, privately agreeing to some extent, but feeling something lacking in the diagnosis.

The Italian shrugged. "No underlying physical cause that can be determined by these tests. You say she performed well on the neuro exams given when she emerged from the coma. I believe the lethargy to be psychosomatic in nature. Do you not?"

"I do." Nick had come to the same conclusion. "May we keep her here overnight?"

"She has not been officially admitted. We would need to do that."

Nick gritted his teeth. "I explained that this is not an option. She must remain anonymous."

"Do not think me uncooperative, Dr. Sandro," Purpura almost pleaded. "Your...associate, this Mercier..."

"Will see that you are properly thanked and reimbursed for your trouble. As for my patient, I'll take her home now."

But he couldn't take her to his apartment. They had been traced there once. Somehow. Even though the men who had found them were dead now, who knew where their employer was and how much he knew about the location? No, he would have to drive her all the way back to Aunt Sophia's where he knew she would be safe.

A nurse came with a wheelchair and Nick used it to take Cate to the building's entrance, planning to wheel her all the way to the car.

But it was already there. Eric Vinland was sitting in the driver's seat of the stolen vehicle, which he'd parked six feet from the steps. "How is she?" he asked, getting out to help Nick with Cate.

"Tests look okay. What are you doing here? And how did you…"

"Jack called. I was the closest so I came right away." He opened the back door of the car and watched as Nick got Cate settled in the backseat. She fell asleep instantly. "You look sort of peaked. Bad night, huh?" he said to Nick.

Nick didn't bother to answer the obvious. "Let's go."

"In a minute. About her diagnosis…"

"That, I am not going to discuss with you," Nick said firmly.

Vinland rolled his eyes and shook his head, obviously exasperated. "Well, let me ask you this then. What do you call it when there's no physical reason for not being able to do something, but you can't do it anyway? I mean, when you're not faking it, but really can't?"

Nick squinted over at him. "Conversion disorder."

"Yeah. You're thinking that's what she's got. Like when a person goes blind or deaf after something happens. It's like that?"

"And where'd you get your medical degree?" Nick asked, not bothering to hide his sarcasm.

Vinland grinned, teeth flashing. "Hey, you're the doc. I was only adding my two cents' worth to the diagnosis you're considering. Neither one of us can know for sure unless we figure out what's going on in that complicated mind of hers. I can't connect with her when she's not letting herself think. So first thing in the morning, you have to get her thinking."

"*Connect* with her?" Nick asked with a humorless laugh. "Oh God, don't tell me."

"Okay."

"Just get in your car and drive. We ought to go before I shut down myself if you don't mind."

Nick thought about their conversation for the entire hour and a half it took to clear the city and get to his aunt's villa. If only it were as easy as Vinland thought it was to get inside someone's mind.

Once they arrived, Vinland helped Nick get Cate out of the car and up to her bedroom. After Nick shot him a warning look, he stood back, hands-off, and watched as Nick took off her shoes.

Nick settled Cate in her bed while making a mental list of the things he had to check first thing. He brushed her hair off her brow, automatically checking for fever, though he admitted it was only an excuse to touch her face.

"Let her sleep," Vinland said from the doorway. "We have to talk before I take off."

Reluctantly, Nick left Cate and went downstairs with him to Sophia's library. "What's so important?"

"Cate's important," Vinland told him. "You're pretty sure this particular problem isn't physical, aren't you?"

"None of the tests indicate that it is." Nick pointed Vinland into Sophia's library. "I shouldn't be discussing Cate's condition with a nonfamily member and certainly not with one of her coworkers."

"Anything that affects her safety or well-being is crucial for us to know. You know the agency's been cleared by her family to receive all reports on her health. Besides our personal concern for her, Cate's privy to a boatload of information that's highly classified. That has to stay protected."

"She's not exactly divulging secrets, Vinland."

"No, but it's a rule. Anytime an agent is not in full control of her faculties, such as sedated for surgery and later in recovery, another agent has to be present to see that they reveal nothing. To tell you the truth, we thought she was totally lucid or one of us would have been detailed to stay with her at all times. So I need to know you can get her on track in a hurry."

Nick sighed. "Any report I made on Cate at this point would be preliminary." He needed to determine cause and treatment. Conversion disorder happened because the patient needed the disability to avoid doing something they dreaded or felt was impossible.

"It was dread, then," Vinland said, nodding. "Cate doesn't believe anything's impossible."

Nick's eyes flew open in surprise. Then he quickly snapped them shut. He did *not* want an explanation. He just didn't want to hear that Vinland could read his thoughts. It was not possible.

"Cate's right, you know," Vinland insisted. "About nothing being impossible."

Nick suddenly felt an inexplicable wave of apprehension wash through him. This whole conversation was ripping him out of his comfort zone. He had never believed in psychic phenomena. And yet...

"You'll do anything to help her," Vinland said, his tone taking on an urgent note. "You said you would and I know you meant it."

"Anything," Nick assured him.

"Good, because you're going to have to. It will be up

to you to get inside her mind and determine how to fix what's wrong. You have to do it. I can't stay."

"Don't tell me what I *have* to do! And what do you mean, you can't stay? You just told me it was required!"

"Special circumstances. We're going to have to trust you."

Nick could see the agent now faking a calmness he didn't feel, maybe for his own sake, maybe for Nick's. But the best thing Vinland could do for Nick's peace of mind was stick around and help guard Cate. "Where are you going?"

Vinland's lips tightened and he shook his head before he answered. "Back to Florence. Adin's in country."

"Here? In Italy?" Nick demanded. "I thought you said he was in Germany!"

"He was, but I guess he heard about your shoot-out. That means there was somebody left alive out of that hit squad to inform him. I was back in Florence trying to track him down through some of my contacts when I got the call from Jack about Cate. I have to find Adin before he finds her."

"We were careful not to leave a trail of any kind. He won't find her in an out-of-the-way place like Aunt Sophia's villa."

Vinland shot Nick a meaningful look. "I did."

Nick shook his head. "I know about that implanted tracking device. She told me."

"Jack didn't give me that information when he ordered me to come by and check on her. It was a test to see how easily she could be located by others. It took me less than twelve hours."

"So she's not safe here."

Vinland shrugged. "Safe as she would be anywhere. With these people, there's really no perfect place to hide. Just stay aware, that's all I'm saying."

Chapter 8

Nick propped his arm against the mantel and a foot on the hearth as he watched Vinland pace for a minute.

He seemed intense now, all signs of his usually amused attitude and his patently fake calmness missing. Suddenly he sat down and leaned forward in one of the leather chairs beside the fireplace, elbows on his knees as he gestured at Nick with his hands.

His laser gaze held Nick's as he spoke. "You're an easy subject to read. That means your path is open even if it is a one-way street right now. For Cate's sake, we have to change that, Doc, and we have to do it pretty damn quick."

Nick grunted a wry laugh. "Right."

Vinland pointed to the chair opposite the one where he sat.

"Sit, prop your feet up. And for God's sake, get receptive. I don't have time to dick around. You *can* do this, Sandro."

Nick sat, crossed his feet on a matching leather hassock, linked his hands over his chest and squinted at Vinland. "Do what? Become psychic? Are you serious?"

"Yeah."

"That's a pretty large claim. So why not do whatever you plan to do on Cate herself?"

"She had it and lost it. Nothing I can do will restore that if she's not ready or able. And trust me, she's not."

"Trust you? I don't even believe you."

"Close your eyes and think something. Anything."

Nick sighed. *Like who does this jerk-off think he is? Like maybe this whack job should be the one reclining with his eyes closed and getting analyzed?*

"I've been analyzed to death, thanks," Vinland retorted to Nick's unspoken thought. "And I'm no jerk off." He offered a tight smile. "Not usually anyway."

"My God," Nick whispered, his eyes round with shock. "You…you…"

Vinland nodded. "Yeah, I did. Now if you'll cooperate, I'll tell you what to do. This works. I've done it with several of our agents, helping them enhance their abilities. If you're a good broadcaster, then you can do a probe and receive. Almost everyone has the innate ability to connect psychically, or at least empathetically. Getting feelings is almost as good as words, but we'll try for both."

"That's bull!" Nick declared.

"No, it's not. Only sci-minded types like you who insist on locked-down empirical evidence don't buy it. And of course the masses who let it go unused refuse to acknowledge it's real." His vehemence softened a little. "Many who *can* do it never admit to it and you can see why not. It works to their advantage to keep it to themselves."

Nick frowned up at him. "Unless they've heard of that guy offering a cool million to anyone who could prove the existence of such things!"

Vinland smiled. "Some things are worth more than a million, Doc. Take my word, this is one of them. It's a major tool in doing my job. Think how valuable this will be when you set up as a shrink."

Nick couldn't deny it. Neither could he envision himself breaking into minds for hidden secrets. It didn't seem right.

"Don't go prudish on me, Doc. Let's get on with it. You can use this or not when that time comes. You *can* turn it off and on when you find the buttons. But you *must* use it with Cate."

"I couldn't do that! I mean, even if I *could*, I wouldn't."

Vinland brushed aside his objection. "Get her thinking again, locate the problem and fix it. It will mean the difference in her ability to hold a job whether she works for us or not." He let out a sigh. "And frankly, we could use her help with configuring the extent of Adin's reach as soon as she's able to handle it."

Nick nodded, still overwhelmed by Vinland's proven ability and the idea that he might possess it himself. Surely not, but what could it hurt to try? He'd feel like a fool if this were a joke, but so what?

"All right, do your worst." He leaned back and closed his eyes. "You want me to think something else?"

"No. Mind blank as you can make it. Consciously relax every muscle. Begin with your feet and work up," Vinland ordered in a normal voice and waited for Nick to comply. Then he began to speak more softly, his words becoming dronelike.

Ah, hypnosis. Others had tried. It was too bad he couldn't be hypnotized. That was Nick's last lazy thought before he allowed himself to drift away into nothingness.

He woke when sun through the window crept across his face. Morning. With a heavy sigh, he sat up and stretched, squinting as he looked around the room.

The memory of last night rushed at him and he got to his feet. Vinland was gone. Aunt Sophia stood in the doorway. "Coffee is ready. Cate is having hers in her room if you wish to join her."

"How…how is she?" Nick asked, rubbing his eyes. His body felt relaxed, almost numb, but his mind was in turmoil.

Sophia inclined her head. "Not well, I think. She seems afraid, nervous. So unlike her, isn't it?"

Nick was already past his aunt and headed up the stairs, Vinland's foolishness and Sophia's offer of coffee forgotten.

Cate sipped the strong, sweet brew and tried to recall the events of last night. She did remember the episode with the computer yesterday and how frightened she'd been. After that, things were as blurred as the words she'd tried to read and couldn't.

She should be more upset by that than she felt, Cate thought. Had Nick given her something to sedate her?

It seemed he had taken her to a hospital for tests, but maybe that was a mixed-up flashback to Switzerland since here she was in her bed this morning.

Obviously, she'd had some kind of setback with her recovery. A strange sort of energy welled inside her. She knew she should be worried about it, but at the moment, she wasn't.

Nick burst into the room. "Cate?"

"Hi, Nick," she said, smiling up at him from her soft nest of lace-trimmed pillows. She held up her cup. "Coffee?"

She watched as he drew in a deep breath and visually checked her out, head to toe. The heat in his eyes aroused her. *Unbearably.*

"Want to join me?" She set the cup on the bedside table and threw back the coverlet. Odd, she was still wearing the velour jogging suit she'd had on yesterday.

Nick's eyebrows drew together in a worried frown.

Cate lowered her eyelashes and raised them again slowly. "I guess you're not a morning kind of guy."

Now she had shocked him, she realized. No wonder. She had shocked herself. Maybe what she'd glimpsed in his expression had been concern, not heat at all. God, what was wrong with her?

The feelings rushing through her were scary, like she had no control over them. The insistent ache inside her crushed pain and pleasure together. Her body vibrated with the dire need to have him, feel him all around her, within her, to forget about any and everything but him and what he could give her.

"God, this suit is hot!" She dragged off the jacket. Underneath she wore only a silk tank top. Frantically, she tossed off the covers and peeled the pants down her legs and kicked them off.

"Cate?" Nick sounded really worried now.

"Lust," she whispered, confused, afraid and defensive, catching and holding his gaze. "I know it's not right."

"What?" He shook his head as if to clear it and was seriously frowning at her now.

"Inappropriate *lust!*" she exclaimed. "Don't you get it? Something's wrong." It sure was. Strong desire for him wasn't the real problem, however. She'd always had that. Her inability to control it was. She burned and felt consumed by it.

He approached and sat on the edge of the bed. His hand cradled her face and Cate leaned into his touch, relishing the feel of his skin against hers.

As she did, she noticed rapid changes in Nick over the next few seconds. His expression altered from worry to sudden surprise. He started to get up, then slowly sat back down.

The shocked look on his face slowly yielded to a quiet confidence she recognized as the Nick she knew best. And maybe there was an underlying hum of excitement in his eyes, too. Yeah, he was a doctor and he liked putting the facts together. She hoped to hell he had because she didn't know what was going on.

"Don't let this upset you, Cate. It's just another symptom. Like the dizziness and balance problem."

"Not *quite,*" she declared, totally unsettled. She crossed her arms over her breasts to hide the evidence of their wicked anticipation. "So what do we do about it? Exercise?"

Cate felt like writhing in the bed—with him—but she held still, knowing there was only one way to assuage the need she was feeling. And the doctor wouldn't be willing to fill *that* prescription. At least not now or under these circumstances.

She wanted to grab him and kiss that look off his face. Anger and frustration were rapidly replacing the desire. Good! She jerked away from his touch and he sat back, simply observing her for a few minutes.

Now he was wearing his distant doctor expression. "You look condescending," she accused. "And you'd better not be."

"We have to address this. It's important."

"Well, unless you *feel* randy, I hope you've got a pill for it," she snapped, tucking her chin to her chest and avoiding his eyes. "I'm bloody miserable!"

"I'll send for something, don't worry. First, let's talk about what we're dealing with."

"I *told* you what we're dealing with! I am well aware of it. Got that?"

He ignored her. "Some changes in the brain are microscopic, especially true with diffuse axonel injury. This could be physical."

"Yeah, it is definitely *physical,* okay?" She huffed impatiently. "Doctorese is not one of my languages. Speak English."

"Don't play dumb, Cate," he said, shaking his head. "All right, here's the layman's version. Most of your problems lie with motor deficits, like your balance, decreased endurance, delays between thinking something and doing it. You have a couple of perceptual problems, the double vision, heightened sensation in…some of your body parts."

She rolled her eyes. "You *think?*"

He smiled, obviously glad she was not acting on her impulses. "Your functional capabilities are probably better than anyone figured at first. Do you realize you perform almost normally when you don't think about it so much?"

"*Almost* being the key word there. I've lost my job, at least the one I was hired to do. And now I feel like I'm going to be reduced to lap dancing if you don't do something."

He nodded. "I will. If it's any consolation, I don't think this is due to damaged brain cells, not directly at any rate. These feelings you're having now are just an attempt at compensating for what you fear you can no longer do. Your mind wants to substitute sex. It feels good, gives you distraction and fulfills the old repro instinct that gives us all a sense of worth. See it for what it is and it will diminish."

She puffed out her cheeks and shook her head as she released a breath of frustration. "Easy for you to say."

"I think that your lack of acceptance, not your injury, is causing this and the reading problem, too. One reason I believe it's psychosomatic is that you were tested before and had no reading deficit. Then you went on the computer yesterday and you did. And this overactive libido is just as new."

Little did he know. "So you're telling me I'm crazy?"

"There's nothing crazy about it, Cate. Your brain is trying hard to fix itself. Now then, think what you were about to do at the computer, and why putting that into motion would generate fear."

Cate avoided his eyes. "You keep using that word, *fear,* and I am *not* afraid!"

How could she tell him she'd meant to check out the diagnosis and prognosis he and the other doctors had agreed on? He'd think she didn't trust him at all. She had planned on looking for some loopholes in their logic, some argument against their certainty that she wouldn't completely recover.

"All right, Cate. I get it. I really do," he said, touching her leg. She quickly moved it. He looked at her long and hard before he continued. "You were afraid of what you might find on that computer when you began to search."

"Damn it! No!"

Again he stared at her, his eyes narrowed, focused like lasers. Angry? She shouldn't have snapped at him. That made her look even more unbalanced. "Sorry," she said. "I'm just edgy this morning."

"I know, and that's understandable," he replied. "Tell you what. I'm going to get you some medication to help with your symptoms. Meanwhile, you just rest. Get some sleep if you can. You had a busy night. But you are better this morning. Much better."

Cate wanted to ask him exactly what *had* happened, but she didn't want him to know she didn't recall most of it.

He stood up, then leaned down. To kiss her, maybe? She moved away, avoiding him just in case.

If he touched her in any way right then, she felt she would explode. The problem was, she didn't know what form that explosion would take. She wanted to grab and ravish him. She wanted to hit him over the head. She wanted to cry all over him and beg him to make her well. God only knew which direction she'd take if she didn't avoid him altogether.

Cate saw he had only been leaning toward the bedside table to pick up her coffee cup. He offered it to her, but she refused, not even wanting their fingers to touch.

She guessed he realized exactly what she was feeling when he walked away from her bed and turned at the door. "Try concentrating on something totally unrelated to sex, your injury or your work. Something calm and peaceful."

She scooted down in the bed and yanked the covers over her head. "Just get out of here, will you? Leave me alone!"

The door closed softly behind him. She heard it click.

Oh, man, she could not afford to be this mentally messed up. Nick wouldn't let her do anything insane when it came to personal or medical matters. He obviously knew how to handle all that, thank goodness. But somebody was gunning for her and they might strike again before she could get her head straight.

What if they discovered where she was? What if Nick tried to get between her and whoever came after her next? He might not be as lucky as he'd been in Florence.

She had to pull herself together and get as efficient as possible as quickly as she could in order to protect Nick,

Aunt Sophia and herself. Nobody in this house, or even in the area, was trained to deal with threats like that but her.

Paranoia. Another symptom? Nope, as the old saying went, they really *were* out to get her. That was a fact.

With all the effort she possessed, Cate pushed that worry aside and tried to come up with something nonthreatening to think about as Nick had instructed. Unfortunately, even her childhood held very few memories of anything calm, and all of those peaceful incidents were related to him, to his influence and presence as she grew from wild child to woman. Like dwelling on those times would help her now?

It wasn't a blow to her brain that made her want him like crazy. All that had done was loosen her inhibitions and make her forget the reasons why she couldn't have him. At the moment, none of those reasons made any sense.

Nick sat down on the top stair tread and lowered his face to his palms. He couldn't believe he had read her thoughts without even trying. And that he hadn't told her what he was doing. God, this was too much to take in all at once.

Cate's mind had opened to him like a book. He felt guilty as hell for the intrusion. Damn Vinland. And bless him, too. Thanks to him, Nick knew the reason Cate had lost her ability to read. He could fix that in time. Maybe his identifying the cause would do that for her.

Now he understood what Vinland had meant about having a perfectly valid reason for holding the ability secret. It was a terrible and valuable thing to possess. He also saw how it could be misused and wondered just how many people did employ it for gain.

He hadn't discovered the trigger to activate it. That had just happened and had taken him completely off guard. Looking at her intently might have done the trick. He needed to find that switch, though. Otherwise he couldn't turn it off at will.

That worry aside, he pulled out the cell phone Mercier had provided and made a call. He rattled off the required medication and was assured it would be delivered within a couple of hours. He wondered how and by whom, but Mercier hadn't failed them so far. The man had power, that was for sure.

For the present, Cate was safe, probably sleeping again. In any case she would feel a lot more comfortable if he stayed out of her bedroom.

He went downstairs to find Aunt Sophia and see whether his newfound mind-reading ability worked with her as well as it had with Cate. On the way, he grimaced at his plan. So much for an altruistic use of his new gift— using his lovely old aunt as a test subject.

He imagined he could hear Vinland's laughter. Was the sonofabitch reading him right now from a distance? Could that be done? Damn, he had to figure out a way to block others out if possible. And he needed to do some serious research on this.

That was when it occurred to him that Cate really had been reading *him* for years when they were growing up. She'd even told him so, knowing full well he didn't believe her. Payback shouldn't be occurring to him at this point, but it did. At least it helped with his guilt.

The tables were turned now. Cate could no longer tell

what he was thinking. Thank God for that! When he'd first
seen her there, all cuddled into the covers and inviting him
in, he had totally forgotten for a second their doctor/patient
relationship. He hoped that brief aberration had been due
to his relief at finding her lucid and not semicatatonic as
she'd been last night.

He had nearly ignored the real reason for her coming
on to him the way she had. God help him, he had considered, just for a split second, taking her up on the offer. He
wanted her that bad. Wrong, inappropriate and highly un-
professional of him, but there it was.

The only saving grace about his feelings for her was
that it wasn't only her body he craved. Cate was everything he admired. No other woman he'd ever known
could compare to her, his courageous, funny, exasperat-
ing and outrageous Cate.

Every protective instinct he possessed had kicked into
overdrive when she was threatened. She was at risk on two
fronts already. Now he had to protect her from himself,
too. And he would, damn it. He meant to do everything
within his power as a man to keep her safe and all within
his skill as a physician to help her regain her skills.

However, what if he managed to correct her other
deficits and that psychic ability came back to her in the
process?

What if they both had it at the same time? Emotional
chaos and a vulnerability neither of them had yet experienced might cause a disaster. Or maybe an intimate connection that could blow both their minds.

Chapter 9

"Aunt Sophia, I need to talk to you," Nick said when he found her in the kitchen.

She smiled as she raised a spoon to taste the sauce she was cooking.

Nick focused on her quick, dark eyes as they met his. The anticipation in them struck him first, only as a feeling, no particular words, but it was a stronger impression than he would have gleaned merely from studying her expression.

Yes, you can do it. Your friend was right. I listened to you two last evening. Did it work with Cate?

Nick's leg bumped the stool he stood next to and he sat down abruptly. He leaned on the island, watching her as she stood across from him, stirring her sauce. "Can *you?*" he asked.

"Read your mind?" She grinned and inclined her head. "Perhaps. Do you think so?"

He drew in an unsteady breath and scraped a hand over his face. "This…this is all too new. I'm having trouble grasping it."

"Nonsense," she replied evenly. "You have been doing it to some extent throughout your life, dear boy. You know, with patients, your parents, friends, certainly Cate. You sensed what they needed and acted upon that."

"How on earth would you know that? We've known each other what, three months? You never saw me with any of them other than Cate."

Her expression became serious then. "You have always done as others expected, as you knew would please them. Even with your wife, I am sure you did this."

Nick huffed out a mirthless laugh. "Yeah, right." But he supposed he had empathized to a certain extent, there at the end of his marriage at any rate. He had understood that she wanted out of the marriage and why. Karen had needed more from him than was possible for him to give. She hadn't had to say it out loud, so maybe he had read her thoughts. Maybe she had read his, too, or at least sensed that he'd felt his heart was somewhere else. With Cate, of course. If he was honest with himself, he had always loved her. Only her. There had been no period of blame, self-examination or grief over his mistakes or Karen's. No anger, just understanding of the simple mistake they had made and how to fix it without any useless recriminations. They remained friends. "Maybe you're right."

"Of course I am. Now you must accept this ability you have and use it wisely. To answer your question, no, I cannot do what you are doing. I am merely an old woman who sees what she sees and knows what she knows." Again she grinned at him. "But perhaps I shall try to improve on these skills after hearing all that your friend had to say on the subject."

Nick felt a calmness and satisfaction steal over him. This was nothing to be afraid of, nothing so weird he ought to reject it. Vinland hadn't shoved this into his head by force, it had been there all along, suppressed by his skepticism, waiting to be released.

You are freeing yourself from other repressing beliefs and becoming the man you were meant to be, my nephew.

Nick startled, his gaze flying to meet Sophia's. "I wasn't looking at you!"

"No, but you heard my thoughts because I sent them to you," she admitted. "Like an e-mail message." She tapped the spoon on the edge of the pot. "Hit *Send!*"

Nick laughed, almost giddy. Or maybe hysterical. "Just like that? Then I need to find a way to log off mind mail or I could be overrun with spam."

She pursed her lips and nodded. "Just so."

Somehow Nick didn't think there were any programs available over the counter and no free download to prevent unwanted thoughts from invading his mind. "I guess there's a downside to this. Vinland mentioned a switch I had to find for myself."

Sophia held out the spoon full of sauce. "Here, use another of your senses and tell me if there is enough seasoning."

Nick did as she asked, humming his approval of her efforts. He thought about his other senses as he did it.

"Insignificant sounds like traffic noise or singing birds are usually screened out automatically unless you actively listen for them," he said, testing a theory. "Or unless a particularly significant sound intrudes. That's why the hard of hearing have such problems adjusting to hearing aids. Everything's amplified equally."

She tore off a piece of the homemade loaf on the breadboard and handed it to him. "And you can replace the taste of one thing by substituting another." She shrugged one shoulder. "Same with touch. It is difficult to register two textures at once, isn't it?"

"I think so." He took a bite of the bread and chewed, enjoying the yeasty flavor as he thought. "You close your eyes to shut out unwanted sights. But when you do look, you can only focus on one object at the time. Things around it are seen, yet blurred until you refocus on something else." He thought he had it now. "That's the key. Focus is the key. At least until the screening becomes automatic!"

Sophia pointed at him with the sauce-covered spoon. "And practice makes perfect. So go along now and leave me to my cooking. Find another guinea pig."

Nick walked around the kitchen island and kissed Sophia's cheek. "You are such a doll. If I ever have a daughter, I will name her Sophia and hope she turns out exactly like you."

"Not if, but *when*," Sophia replied with a tinkling laugh. "But I expect your little Sophie will be much taller than I, considering Cate's height."

Nick had to laugh. "You aren't going to give up on making a match between us, are you?"

"No," she admitted, raising her eyebrows in a knowing way. "And neither will you if you are as smart as I think you are." She shooed him away with her apron. "Now go! I have pasta to make and that requires concentration."

When Cate was better, Nick thought they might finally get together, at least for long enough to get each other out of their systems. Their mutual attraction had been brewing too long not to come to some sort of cataclysmic conclusion if they stayed together long enough.

For now, however, it was hands-off. Cate wasn't up to anything but working on her recovery.

So, one thing at a time, then, Nick concluded as he went in search of another subject on whom to test his new *gift*. He had begun to see it as just that, a remarkable gift.

There weren't many around. Cate's agency had run checks on everyone who worked at the villa, Mercier had told him. Sophia had dismissed almost all her staff and sent them home with full pay. Exceptions were the head gardener, Armando, and a handyman, Pietro. Apparently, they refused to leave Sophia alone with the "strangers." Nick suspected those two also served as his aunt's bodyguards since the villa was fairly isolated, at least a mile from the village.

Both men had worked here for decades, were in their sixties, still built like bulls. Neither had been very talkative in the few days he and Cate had been around, but Nick had been too busy to try to get acquainted. Now was the time.

* * *

Cate took the pills Aunt Sophia brought her and waited for them to take whatever effect they were supposed to. An hour later, she didn't feel any different at all. Placebos, she suspected. However, the keen edge of arousal had already subsided before the medication arrived, so it didn't matter.

She had begun to process all that Nick had told her about her condition. Maybe she simply didn't know how to recognize fear and couldn't handle it in the usual way. Oh, she had been scared a few times in her life, but her response to it was to face whatever made her cringe and brave it out. Nobody ever saw her sweat.

Running from something was only a means to stay alive and gain a position from which to fight. This was a mind thing, that was true, but she didn't see why it shouldn't be handled in the same way. What other way was there?

Tomorrow, she promised herself, she would face her devils. For now, she only wanted to sleep.

The next morning Cate woke slowly, rubbing her eyes and squinting at the clock on the mantel across the room. Five o'clock, just like old times. Coincidental, of course, and nothing to do with her internal clock kicking in, but it seemed like a sign. She sat up in bed and stretched.

Back home, she'd get up at five, exercise for half an hour, shower, get dressed, eat breakfast and be off to work by half past six. Only now there was no job to go to. And the rest of the house was still asleep. Even Nick didn't rise this early.

This seemed like a good thing to do, getting back into her old routine. She slid out of bed, pulled on her robe against the chill of the drafty room and padded barefoot to the bathroom. It was as picturesque as the rest of the place, but a lot newer, fashioned probably in the thirties, judging from the large dressing room between her room and Nick's. She was careful to be quiet so she wouldn't wake him.

Right on her old schedule, she did her stretches and the other exercises that Nick recommended. Then she pulled on jeans, a sweater and the running shoes Nick had given her and went downstairs.

Lights were on in the kitchen and she found Sophia sitting at the table with a cup of coffee. "Good morning," Cate said.

"You are awake early."

"I slept almost all day yesterday. You'd think I'd be groggy." Cate poured herself a cup of the strong, fragrant brew, added the heavy cream from the pitcher and pulled out a chair. "Maybe I needed the sleep. I feel different this morning. Better," she added.

"Perhaps it is the medicine Nick ordered for you. He is a wonderful doctor, don't you think?"

Cate smiled. "Sure he is."

She still had to take it slowly whenever she turned her head or her vision would blur. However, she was definitely more stable, her legs stronger and her back straighter. And best of all, she felt more clearheaded and alert than she had since the accident. Only now did she realize there had been this fog of unreality.

"But I think you must, how do you say? *Fire* him," Sophia announced. She sliced off a piece of the crusty loaf in front of her, spread it with a delicious local cheese and passed it to Cate.

"*Fire* him? Why?" Cate asked, taking the offering and biting into it with relish.

Sophia shrugged one shoulder and set about preparing her own breakfast. "He will never mix business with pleasure. That is the way he is. He is your doctor or your lover, but never both at once, you see."

Cate laughed. "You've got him pegged, that's for sure."

Sophia smiled, her gaze shifting from Cate to some memory. "I had a physician once. My first husband. Ah, he was magnifico, my Andreas. I dream of him still."

"A real catch, huh? How did you meet?"

"We worked together during the war. And after. Nick is very like him." She winked at Cate. "And I believe you are much like me."

"So you think we're meant to be together because of that. What if we don't love each other?"

Sophia threw up her hands and shook them, a patent gesture of exasperation. "Why do people find this question of love so confusing?" she demanded. "Why is that? A man holds your life and happiness dearer than his own, then he loves you! You feel the same about him, you love him. As clear as new glass!"

"That simple, huh? Andreas was like that, was he?"

Sophia lowered her hands and crossed them over her heart. "He died for me, that man. Believing us both doomed, he died to give me only a moment more of life."

"I'm so sorry," Cate said sincerely. She saw the love and survivor's guilt in Sophia's tears.

The old woman shrugged a shoulder. "Such is life. I have loved since, but never so deeply." Her eyes met Cate's. "Nicholas could have run from all of this after you left Florence, you know. Everything he has done there and since runs counter to his training and his way of life. He has never been a part of your world of danger and yet he embraces it, despite that. You must ask yourself why."

Why, indeed. Honor, duty, a secret lust for adventure and new experience? Who knew? He'd never said he loved her, only that he cared about her.

Cate had always resented the way her parents and Nick's pushed them at each other. So had he. But she found Sophia's matchmaking oddly sweet.

Sophia had left the table and was looking out the window at the sunrise. "Today will be a beautiful day," she said as if ordaining it herself. "Warm for this time of year."

"Like to take a walk with me?" Cate asked as she joined her to gaze over the beauty of rolling Tuscany with its stripes of grape vines and heavy dottings of fluorescent trees interspersed with evergreens. Fog still hung in places, already burned away in others. A gorgeous, otherworldly landscape viewed from high on this hill.

"Wait for Nicholas," Sophia suggested, turning from the window and returning to the table.

Cate thought how long she had waited for him already and hadn't even known that was what she had been doing. But what did she really want from him if she could have him? Marriage, the picket fence, children? Hardly. That wasn't her. It obviously wasn't him, either. A wild fling? Friends with privileges? That made her laugh.

But what else *was* there? Maybe that last thought wasn't such an outrageous idea, after all.

This was no decision to be made in a hurry, though. In fact, she didn't want to make any big decisions today and she didn't want to think about anything troubling when she felt this good. Not the issue of losing her ability to read, not the possibility of Adin finding her, not the question of whether she would recover completely or the loss of the work she loved. She would enjoy the day, that was all.

She concentrated only on small things all day long, smelling the roses, as it were. She made bread with Sophia, a brand-new experience for her. After that, touring the other rooms of the villa by herself and imagining what they had been like two centuries ago when the place was new.

Nick was all doctor whenever they were together, which wasn't often. She figured she had really given him a scare. He spent a lot of time outdoors, talking with Sophia's help. Assessing the security around the house, he'd told her at dinner. They all retired early and Cate fell asleep instantly with a great feeling of well-being, despite all her problems.

It wasn't until the next morning that she got up, went downstairs and headed directly to the computer. The pad she had written on still lay beside it. Scribbles and dots. Frowning at her former efforts, Cate picked up the pen and took a deep, calming breath. Deliberately, she put it to the paper.

"What are you doing?" Nick demanded as he entered the room.

Cate stopped and turned. "I have to know."

"It might be too soon," he warned. "Failure will reinforce your fear."

"And success will eliminate it, right?"

He pulled up a footstool and sat next to her. That placed her in the dominant position, which she knew he intended. That should have annoyed her, but it didn't. There was no hint of condescension in his eyes, only his usual concern.

Why did he have to look so damned desirable? She had to make a fist to keep from reaching out to stroke his face. Her other hand nearly snapped the pen she was holding. She really, really, *really* wanted to kiss him.

The pills weren't working very well if they were supposed to stifle her libido. However, this was not the painful, driving need she had felt the day before yesterday. It was only the reaction she usually had to Nick when he was near.

She sucked in a deep breath and tried not to look at him. Impossible, when he was so close and obviously wanted her to.

Nick radiated confidence and absolute conviction. He had a hell of a bedside manner. His concern and caring were very real. That added tons to his appeal, both as a doctor and a man. She didn't have to imagine the effect he had on female patients. Hell, she was one, and his effect on her right now made her feel a little shallow.

Good looks could be deceiving, but she *knew* Nick, really knew him as a person. There wasn't a deceptive cell in his body. She had been inside that mind of his when he was just a high-school kid, and even then his principles and his goals in life had been set.

So why was she questioning his judgment and his advice?

For a long moment, he said nothing. Man, she wished she could read his thoughts. His expression was a mix of emotions that looked as chaotic as hers felt.

"It's brave of you to come down here and try this, Catie," he said, inclining his head toward the computer. "But I think it's still too soon."

He took her fisted hand in his, opened it and massaged it gently. "Look, why don't you give yourself a break? You've been overdoing it with all the physical therapy."

"I took a break yesterday. Now it's time to get on with this, Nick. I'm fine, really."

"I know, but when you try too hard, it actually slows you down. That could prove to be the case here, too. Let things progress naturally. Take another day or two at least."

Cate hesitated. Did she do that because his suggestion made perfect sense or was she giving in to the fear she had yesterday? Was she ready to admit to him that she had been afraid?

"I'm your doctor," he reminded her. "It does make sense to listen to me, don't you think? If you took to heart everything else I told you about your condition, why not believe me about this?"

"I think you're a little too overprotective, that's all," she said, holding his gaze. "I have to know if I can do this. The suspense is killing me."

He smiled. "Patience is the hardest thing for you, always has been, but I'm only asking you to postpone this, not give it up and forget it." His thumb caressed her wrist as his eyes held hers. He shook his head. "Trust me.

Don't do it while your pulse is racing. While you're this anxious about it."

Cate knew he was right. She tossed the pen on the desk. "Okay. Distract me then." *Kiss me. Hold me. Make love to me right here on this fancy Aubusson carpet.*

He shook his head. "Ah, Catie," he said with a sigh that sounded like regret. Then he got up, letting his hand slide from her wrist to grasp her palm. "Coffee's ready. Come have it with Sophia and me."

Cate shook off the buzz of arousal. At least she tamped it down and felt better that she could do that now, even without the medication. The sensation of normalcy had taken hold and it gave her such hope. She felt like her old self. Except for having to move more slowly to keep her eyes working right, she was okay. She glanced again at the computer and decided to humor Nick.

His palm felt hot against hers but he didn't let go of her hand. He clutched it even tighter. Maybe he felt a little jazzed himself, but she knew he wouldn't act on it. Not as long as she was in his care as a patient. Yet another excellent reason to get her edge back. Or maybe she should take Sophia's advice and fire him.

She agreed it might be risky to try the reading thing this soon, but how much time could she afford to waste? Today she had a niggling feeling that danger was closing in. And what made her feel that, she wondered? Had some of her sixth sense returned or was this yet another instance of her brain's synapses misfiring?

Whatever was going on in her head, she had awakened with something warning her pretty insistently. When she did begin seeing words beneath those pictures on the homepage, her time might be better spent clicking on Ahmed Adin's recent activity rather than plundering through medical abstracts on brain injuries.

Back in Florence, Ahmed Adin lost himself in the crowds of tourists on the Ponte Vecchio. He slowly weaved his way past the gold vendors and off the ancient bridge to the shops along the bank. The information he had just obtained proved valuable indeed and no one had noticed the exchange.

He liked to meet his contacts within a sea of people. It was much easier to remain invisible or to disappear if recognized. Duck away, don a hat, discard a jacket. There were so many people here of Middle Eastern descent, as well as plenty of dark Italians, that his physical characteristics were not remarkable.

That had been Sharmad's big mistake in America. She had let herself stand out. She had, probably on purpose, exposed herself to the agent who followed her. Pride had been her only sin.

Ahmed had been proud of her, too. All his life, she had sheltered him, prayed for him, provided him with the love of a mother even though she had been scarcely ten years older. And as a final gift, his beloved sister had offered her life for the cause.

They both had known she would die soon regardless, and he admired her for the sacrifice of her last precious months. It was not only her death he sought to avenge on the woman who had caused it. This agent would remain dangerous, a serious threat to his holy war.

The Olin woman possessed powers of the mind that she used to find those who would undermine her decadent society and destroy its foundation. He knew of this from the notes of the American writer, Sam Jakes, who had researched her. Reporters of all stripes were relentless in their need to expose any and everything. Ahmed had all of the information gathered for that exposé, even facts the man was not allowed or thought unwise to put into print.

Ahmed now knew much about this government agency to which she belonged, a highly covert organization, supposedly. However, they were more or less legend within other, less-secret law enforcement communities.

One of their male agents was seeking Ahmed now, here, within this city. The information received on the bridge a few moments ago was a delightful gift from Allah: the whereabouts of the woman Ahmed wanted dead and also the identity of the agent, Eric Vinland, who had unwittingly provided her location.

This man had once posed as Jared Al-Dayal, a wealthy emirate ostensibly making deals all over the Middle East while actually gathering intelligence for the Americans. No more of that, Ahmed thought with a satisfied smile.

Two birds with one stone. An apt description of the next move Ahmed would make. He could almost thank the greedy Westerners he had hired to complete his vengeance for failing in their task. Everything had happened to lead him to this point in time. Conditions were now perfect for him to effect his plan personally.

Justice for his sister and the eradication of the spy would

make him a legend. Full credit would be his alone. Dedicated followers would flock to him as if he were bin Laden himself.

Tonight he would allow the agent, Vinland, to find him. And he would send a new, more reliable force to bring him the woman.

Chapter 10

The ancient clock in the corner struck midnight. Nick sat alone in the dark in Sophia's library, his fingertips tented beneath his chin, forming a plan for Cate's therapy the following day. They had decided to wait until then to test her reading skills. He had noticed how she avoided looking at anything with print on it.

He reached for the glass of wine he'd brought in and took a sip. Nothing indicated that this was anything more than simple conversion. He knew she would recover from that in time. And her preoccupation and apprehension over it had distracted her from the physical aspects of her recovery. That was probably a good thing. She had moved more easily today. Her coordination seemed almost normal most of the time. Her reactions to stimuli, more immediate than usual. Yes, good.

When his cell phone chirped, he resented the interruption, but answered immediately. He had a call in to her parents and expected it was them returning it. "Sandro here."

"You need to get Cate out of there. Head for Milan. A plane will be waiting and an agent will meet you at the airport entrance to escort you." Mercier's voice sounded urgent.

"What? Why?"

"Vinland's down. He had a fix on Adin and had planned to take him tonight. Something's gone wrong. We've been tracing Eric's tracker and he's been stationary for over an hour and made no contact. That means he's either dead or captured."

"And you think Adin could be forcing him to reveal Cate's location?"

Mercier sighed, the sound ragged. "Eric would never break, but there are other ways. Trust me, you need to move Cate tonight."

"Right away," Nick agreed. "Keep us advised." He was up and running for the stairs before he got the phone back in his pocket.

"Cate, wake up!" He tossed back the covers and shook her shoulder. "Get up, Catie. We have to leave!"

She rolled to her back and rubbed her face with one hand. Squinting up at him, she groaned. "What is it?"

"I'll explain later. Right now, we have to get you out of

here, so get up and get dressed!" He rushed to grab some clothes for her. "Here, put this on."

She peeled the cotton nightgown over her head and tossed it aside without a hint of modesty. Nick tried to look away, but found he couldn't. Bathed in cool, bluish moonlight from the window, she had the look of a smooth statue done in marble, a timeless sculpture that invited touch. His mouth went totally dry.

She snatched the velour sweats from his hand and began tugging them over her long legs. "Shoes!" she ordered, breaking the spell he was under. While he retrieved her running shoes, she pulled on a tank top and zippered hoodie. Nick was already kneeling, trying to work her foot into one shoe.

"What's the deal?" she demanded, taking over his task.

"Adin has your friend in Florence. Mercier says we have to leave. No time to pack." Nick didn't think it would serve any purpose to suggest that Vinland might be dead.

"He has Eric? We can't just leave him to—"

"Yes, we have to. Mercier's people will take care of Vinland. There's nothing we can do for him ourselves." He grabbed her hand. "Let's go. We have to get Sophia out of here, too, in case Adin shows up looking for you."

And how was he going to alert an eighty-year-old woman that her life was in danger without stopping her heart? No help for that, he thought, as he headed for his aunt's bedroom.

She met them at her door in her dressing gown, light from her bedroom casting her in silhouette. "What is happening? I heard—"

"We're leaving, Aunt Sophia. Get your coat. Is there someone in the village you can stay with for a couple of days?"

"I'm not going anywhere!" she exclaimed. "This is my home. I do not leave it." She cleared her throat as if embarrassed by her vehemence. Her voice lowered. "I never leave it."

Oh God, agoraphobia? He didn't want to force her outside, but he would if he had to. "We *are* going," he stated. "All of us. Someone dangerous might come here looking for Cate and I can't leave you."

"Go if you must," she told him calmly. "I vowed many years ago never to run again and I will not."

Cate grabbed Nick's arm and gave it a shake. "She's right. We should make a stand. At least here, we'll be prepared."

"And well armed," Sophia added, nodding sagely.

Cate continued. "On the road, we'd be more vulnerable than we are now. I can't drive or return fire with any promise of accuracy."

"Mercier ordered us to go," Nick argued, though he realized she was right. What if Adin had determined where they were? They might very well be attacked en route to somewhere else. He remembered that harrowing chase in Florence and knew he'd much rather be in a position where they had at least some defense.

Cate acknowledged his warning about Mercier. "Jack assumes I'm not functioning, but believe me, I'm trained to assess the situation and make decisions like this on my own, Nick. We're staying and that's that."

"I trust your judgment," he told her with a firm nod, "and I agree." The change in Cate astounded him, just as it had during that confrontation in Florence. She was all agent in charge right now and knew exactly what she was doing. He could feel her renewed energy like a presence in the room.

She gave him that confident, daring smile he remembered so well from their youth. "Get the weapon Jack provided and the one you took off our friend in the alley. See how much ammo we have left." She looked to his aunt. "C'mon, Aunt Sophie, let's see what you've got in your arsenal. Where do you keep it?"

"There is a special safe in the wine cellar…"

Nick watched Cate carefully as she and his aunt left the room. How odd that this possibility of danger, this threat of attack, was proving to be such good therapy for her. Maybe adrenaline overrode the effects of her injury.

The brain was an awesome mystery, one he had explored inside and out and still didn't fully understand. With a smile and shake of his head, he went to collect the weapons and ammunition.

Cate marveled at the weaponry available. "My God, you could start your own army! Look at this!" She checked out a rare MP38 German submachine gun, laid that down and picked up an old Walther PPK. "Where did you get all these?" There were dozens.

"My late husband collected most of them as the war ended because he always feared another. The poor man had been virtually defenseless during it, you see, and lost everything his family owned except for this house."

"Helpless, was he?" Cate raised an eyebrow as she counted five shiny black Lugers that looked brand new. "I see most of these are German-made."

Sophia inclined her head as she looked at the handguns. "Those are mine, actually."

Cate remembered Nick telling her that Sophia had worked with the Resistance during the war. "Go, Sophie!" she muttered.

Sophia offered a typically Italian shrug. "Pietro keeps everything in excellent condition. I have him clean these every month or so. This chamber is temperature controlled, you see. Very dry."

Also it was a safe haven and relatively comfortable, if a bit cool. Cate opened a wooden box containing ammunition and began sorting. "I'd like you and your men to take shelter down here if there's trouble."

Sophia began to load one of the Lugers, handling it expertly despite fingers gnarled by arthritis. "Not likely, my dear," she replied.

Cate noted how efficiently the older woman worked. "Have you ever fired any of these?" she asked conversationally.

"Every Tuesday when weather permits," Sophia replied. "That is why Pietro is required to clean them. I could do it myself, but it is a tedious task and I would rather make pasta."

Cate laughed, taking some of the larger weapons down from their racks on the wall.

Nick entered with his two pistols. He looked around, speechless.

"Welcome to the candy store," Cate told him, grinning

at his expression. "You want a machine gun or the crossbow?"

He took the ancient wooden artifact she handed him and frowned at it. "This must be worth a fortune!"

"Fifteenth century, an old family piece," Sophia informed him. "Yours if you want it."

Cate handed him an iron-tipped quarrel. "Don't shoot yourself in the foot."

Nick took the stubby arrow and placed it in the bow, cocking it as if he did it every day. He raised the bow and aimed at the far wall of the chamber. "Believe it or not, I could probably put this to better use than a handgun. I took archery at camp."

"Funny the things I don't know about you," Cate said.

Sophia reached for another of the handguns and continued her task. "A bit of mystery about one another is a good thing, no? This will keep your life together interesting."

Life together. Nick's eyes met hers and held them. They shared a wry smile. Cate felt, in that moment, Nick's acceptance of the inevitable. Her own surrender to it coincided with his as if she had never had any other choice. A current of anticipation seemed to flow between them. She wondered what would come of it.

Nothing right now, she was sure of that. Something inside her had changed, though.

Nick stood, tucking one of his pistols into his belt. He slipped the other one into his jacket pocket. "I'm going upstairs to call Mercier. Unless you'd like to do that? He is your boss."

"Was," Cate said evenly, going back to the business at hand. "Sophia, would you hand me that box of ammo? No, the one marked .45 caliber."

Nick put a hand on her shoulder and gave it a squeeze. "I guess we can mark one to-do item off the list."

She shot him a questioning look and met a proud smile. "What?"

He pointed to the cardboard box she was holding un-opened. "You read the label."

Cate laughed, surprised and overjoyed. She stared at the words written in German, a language she knew fairly well. The letters and numbers appeared perfectly normal, only a bit faded with time. She read it aloud, her Deutsch accent atrocious on purpose and making Sophia giggle.

"Hey, you were right. I *was* just crazy," she said to Nick. Then they were all laughing like they hadn't a care in the world. Cate knew she would always hold that moment as one of her happiest.

Later, upstairs and fortified with coffee and Sophia's cinnamon biscuits, Cate phoned Mercier to get an update on Eric and to tell Jack what she had decided to do.

He argued that she should leave, but eventually saw her logic and promised to send backup as soon as possible. The only two local agents who had been guarding Cate were dead, but most of the SEXTANT and COMPASS teams' available resources were already on the way to Florence to get Eric. Control had pinpointed his location from his implanted tracker. He still had not moved.

Cate rang off and shared the conversation with Nick,

thankful that Sophia had already excused herself and gone to bed after alerting her men, Armando and Pietro, to stand watch. Sophia had also put the word out in the village to keep eyes and ears open for anyone arriving by any mode of travel. There was only one road leading to the villa, through the village itself.

Nick had decided that either he or Cate should stay awake just in case there was trouble. They had stationed themselves in Sophia's library, the heavy drapes drawn over the floor-length windows and a fire lit in the fireplace. The soft amber lighting and Old-World charm of the place imbued a sense of security that both knew might prove deceptive. Nerves were on edge.

"Did Mercier say anything else about Adin?"

"No, just that Eric had located and was going after him and suddenly the tracker stopped moving and has stayed stationary for hours. He hasn't checked in." That could only mean one of two things and they both knew it.

"I don't think Eric's dead," Cate declared. "Jack thinks he might be, but I don't believe it." She pounded a fist in her palm. "If only I could…"

"Connect?" Nick asked. "I tried, but I wasn't entirely sure that could be done. You know, from a distance."

Cate's mouth dropped open.

He sighed and lounged back in the cushy leather chair, propping his chin on his fist. "Yeah, he put the whammy on me so I could read you. Do you mind?"

Cate sputtered for a minute, unsure what to say. He had *read* her? Omigod. What had she been thinking?

Nick smiled knowingly. "Nothing weird. Well, if you don't count that spell of inappropriate lust." He grinned at her. "Interesting. In a medical way, you understand."

Cate threw a magazine at him. "That's not fair! You should have told me!"

"So you could stop me? Come off it, Cate. You did it to me for *years*."

"But I told you I was doing it!" she argued.

"Knowing I didn't believe a word you said. You could have proved it at any time by repeating exactly what I'd just been thinking, but you never did. Same as not telling me."

She crossed her arms over her chest. "I can block you!"

"Do it, then," he challenged. "If you can manage that, maybe you can tele-whatever to Vinland."

Cate sighed. "I tried already. No response, or else I'm not able to get the message."

"Maybe he's unconscious," Nick suggested. "Try it on me."

She shrugged. "I did. No go. Looks like you're the only one with the mojo up and running, damn you."

Nick got up and came over to the sofa where she was sitting and joined her. "You seem back to your old self. I guess danger agrees with you."

"Maybe it does. Do you think my symptoms were all in my head, Nick? Could you and the other doctors have been wrong about all of it?"

He shook his head. "Not all. There was damage done and I expect you'll always have some vertigo, maybe slowed responses in some situations. But you seem to be compensating much more quickly than any of us hoped. I do think your most recent symptoms were psychosomatic, though, because they never presented before. There's no further swelling or bleeding or anything else to explain them."

"What you're saying then, is that I'm about as well as I'm going to get?"

"No. I think you'll continue to improve. I've seen a difference since yesterday, but I expect adrenaline has something to do with that."

"I'm not high on it right now," she argued, "and I feel just fine. Not even tired."

"Remarkable, but then, you always were," he said, nodding. He took her hand in both of his, massaging her wrist, her palm and fingers in that soothing way he had.

"Feels so good," she told him, resting her head against the sofa back and closing her eyes. "Is that what they did to your hand in therapy?"

"Uh-huh. Sometimes a human touch is the only thing that helps, don't you think? No machine can duplicate the comfort."

She snuggled closer and sighed, letting her head rest on his shoulder. "Here we are, holding hands. Our mamas would be so proud."

He laughed. "And our dads would be wondering why I wasn't going for second base and an eventual home run."

"They're not the only ones," she teased. "Read my mind."

Suddenly as that, he raised her chin and kissed her. Gently at first, then increasing the pressure, opening her lips to explore. Cate's mind reeled, incapable of coherent thought as she responded with years' worth of pent-up passion.

He finally broke the kiss and rested his forehead against hers. "This is not the time, Cate, but I am *so* tempted. You're driving me crazy."

"Want one of my pills?" she asked, breathless and frustrated. "They aren't working worth a damn for me."

She felt his body shake with silent laughter as he gave her ribs a fond squeeze with both hands. "You *never* say what I expect."

"Mystery makes me interesting. Aunt Sophie said so."

He leaned back and looked into her eyes. "Don't ever change, Catie. No matter how I try to change you, don't ever let me."

"Kiss me again," she whispered. "Make love to me, Nick. We might not have more than tonight."

He groaned as he slid his arms all the way around her and buried his face in her neck. "That is the oldest line ever used to get laid."

"I hear it works."

"Seriously, what are we going to do, Cate? About us, I mean. Have you ever thought about long-term?"

"I don't know," she answered honestly, then added, "but I never buy a pair of shoes without trying them on first."

He released her slowly and lay back on the sofa, head on the curved armrest, one hand over his face. "I'm sure I'd fit."

She laughed, astonished. "Humor? You have a sense of humor! Omigod, I might have to keep you whether you fit or not. Who'd have guessed?"

Nick moved his hand from his face and smiled up at her, his dark eyes reeling her in. "Kiss me, Cate."

She lay down on top of him, fitting her body to his. Elbows propped on his chest, she caressed his face with both hands, playing his sensuous bottom lip with her thumb. She licked her own lips and thought the most salacious thoughts she could conjure up, wild images of them together in bed doing things she had never done with another man.

He groaned again and she felt the strong evidence of his arousal beneath her. Evidence that he was sharing her every thought and fantasy. Deliberately, she moved against him, thoroughly enjoying his obvious need. Teasing him unmercifully and loving the control she had.

"So what are you thinking now?" she asked in a growling whisper very near his mouth.

"That you're about to try me on," he answered, nipping at her lips and catching them in another mind-bending kiss. She threw herself into it, using every wile she owned to make sure he didn't stop.

He shifted her a little and slid out from under her and onto the plush carpet, pulling her down on top of him. Again, he kissed her, this time with an urgency that exceeded hers. His hands slid beneath her pullover and unsnapped her bra, freeing her breasts to his touch. How right that felt, she thought with a heavy sigh. Oh, my! Magic fingers. He knew exactly where...

"Umm," he growled, releasing her long enough to pull her sweater over her head and toss it aside. She wriggled out of her pants while he tugged off his shirt. In seconds they had dispensed with clothes and lay entwined and writhing.

Cate thought she would die of pleasure right there on the floor, feeling the smooth hardness of his muscles sliding against hers. She inhaled deeply, loving the very scent of him, the sounds he made deep in his throat when she slid her hands over his body.

She met his heavy-lidded gaze and opened her mind to him as fully as she could, sharing all that she was, wishing she could feel inside his mind as he did hers. She opened herself to him and he surged inside her without hesitation.

For a long moment, he held still, his dark eyes hot as they held hers. And then he began to move. Cate could hardly bear the intensity. More than physical, she thought, so much more. Nick was part of her, always had been, always would be. Tears streaked down her face and dropped onto his, but she never looked away as she met him stroke for stroke. Keen pleasure built, built and crashed over her, over him, but even as she cried out with it, she never looked away.

Spent, naked, somewhat chagrined, Cate finally closed her eyes and allowed herself to melt over him like a puddle of wax.

Jeez, what now?

Nick smoothed his palms slowly over her back, up and down. "We get dressed so we don't spend the night here. Much as I'd love to do that, we don't want to get caught with our pants down."

"Pants *off*," she corrected, disengaging and rolling to one side to gather up her clothes. She untangled his slacks from her sweatpants and searched for her underwear.

"Here," he said, tossing them to her.

Cate sort of turned her back as she quickly pulled on her clothes. She consciously closed her thoughts, hoping that much of her gift still worked. She didn't want Nick to pick up on her doubts about what they had just done and how out of control she felt right now.

Served her right, lording it over him the way she'd done. He was probably going to hate her for forcing his hand this way and try to pretend it had never happened.

They'd go on as before. Her chasing, him dashing just out of her reach, using any excuse not to hook up. Age difference, pushy parents, opposing life goals, doctor/patient relationship. What next? She wondered.

"Marry me?" he mumbled.

Cate's hands stilled on the zipper of her hoodie. She slowly turned to face him. "What did you say?"

"You heard me," he said, looking everywhere but at her.

She huffed and resumed zipping. "Serve you right if I shouted yes and jumped you again. What is this? Doing the right thing? Making an honest woman of me? What century are you living in anyway?"

She staggered to her feet, which were still bare. Where the devil were her shoes? She knelt down again and looked under the sofa. "Let's not go there right now. We have enough to worry about as it is."

He was dressed, just buckling his belt. He replaced the pistol and stepped into his shoes, kicking her missing one closer to her. "You don't do *afterward* too well, do you?"

"Nope. Never have. I boot 'em out soon as they deliver." She shot him a glare. "Do you think I do this on a regular basis?"

He had the grace to say nothing. Didn't even raise a dubious eyebrow, which probably saved his life. She had obviously done this before, if not promiscuously, but so had he. He'd been married, for God's sake.

"That was a mistake," he said with a huffed-out sigh.

"Stop reading me!" she demanded.

"Okay, if you'll drop the act. We made love. You wanted to and I wanted to, so we did it. I should be the one kicking myself, but I'm not. It was the single most earth-shaking event of my life and I don't care if we broke a few rules."

"*Your* rules, not mine."

"Well, stop beating yourself up and quit projecting thoughts on me that I never had! I care about you. I'd love to marry you and take care of…"

"Whoa, whoa, whoa!" she shouted, holding up her palms. "You just back it up there, boy! *Nobody* takes care of me, you got that?"

He bit his bottom lip and nodded.

Oh, he could have had a great comeback there. He had been taking care of her and doing a damn fine job of it. This argument could cost her more than she wanted to lose and she had to end it. She sucked in a deep breath and folded her arms over her heaving chest until she calmed down. "You want first watch?"

Again he nodded.

She threw up a hand. "Fine. I'm going upstairs now. Hot shower, pill, nice nap. You'll stay down here. Any alert, you wake me. Got it?"

"Got it," he replied.

She had almost reached the door when he called to her. "Cate?"

"Yeah?" she answered without turning around.

"I love you. Did I mention that?"

She felt her shoulders droop. "No," she said in a small voice. "I don't believe you did."

And it came too late to count, she thought as she stomped up the stairs. Entirely too late.

Chapter 11

Nick realized he'd blown it. He also found out that when his emotions got tangled, this mind-reading trick Vinland had taught him quit working. He had no clue what she was thinking. Dealing with Cate's temper had always been a problem for him, mainly because it really emphasized their basic differences.

How could anyone that volatile do what she had done for a living? Or was that a prerequisite? Hell, he didn't know what it took, but Vinland and Mercier had said she'd been one of the best agents they had.

Sophia's landline rang and Nick hurried to pick up. *"Prego?"*

The innkeeper in the village identified himself and quickly notified Nick that a car had just been spotted zooming past and was headed for the villa. Nick thanked him and hung up. He rushed to the window, threw back the drapes and opened it. "Armando! Pietro! Someone's coming."

They answered and he saw their shadows move around to the loggia. Both were armed with MP38 assault weapons, locked and loaded. He only hoped they had some experience in using them. He closed the window and hurried to wake Sophia and Cate.

Cate was just out of the shower, wrapped in a towel.

"Get your clothes on, car approaching. Take Sophia to the cellar and stay there."

She began grabbing up her clothes and didn't answer him.

"I mean it, Cate. You stay down there!" He couldn't stick around and persuade her. He had to put himself between her and whatever was out there.

They had brought Sophia's most effective weapons up to the kitchen and lined them up on the table, loaded and ready to go. He rushed there and picked up one of the assault rifles Cate had showed him how to use. "Play Al Capone. Point and spray," she had told him. It felt alien in his hands.

Second line of defense was in the foyer. Lights were off inside and out.

"Going down!" Cate called out to him.

"Stay there!" he shouted back, knowing she wouldn't. He'd have to overpower her and tie her to something to keep her in that cellar. She could take him on her worst day, he suspected. He was not trained in hand-to-hand.

Nick listened for the sound of a motor. The men outside must be doing the same. No sounds from them, either. He checked the lock on the front door and moved from the foyer to the library where he pushed open a window. Still nothing.

"You won't hear them."

Nick nearly jumped out of his skin. "God, don't *do* that!"

"Sorry," she muttered, moving up beside him to look outside. "They won't announce themselves, not on purpose anyway. If they're any good at all, they'll attempt to take out our guards and find a way inside that we'll least expect."

"What about Armando and Pietro? I don't think they're up to this. They could be killed."

"They're experienced guards who have seen action. Sophia's late husband didn't hire them for their good looks or gardening skills."

She held the automatic weapon as if it were an extension of herself, an extra appendage she was perfectly used to. Nick tried to copy her stance, but it felt foreign.

"Aunt Sophia settled in down there?" he asked.

"She wanted to stay upstairs and help, but I convinced her we'd have too many cooks in the kitchen if she did."

Nick started to say something, but she quickly shushed him.

"What is it?" he whispered.

"A grunt. Maybe a man down." She backed Nick away from the window, quietly closed and locked it, then motioned him toward the door. "Kitchen," she whispered.

The extra weapons were there and they'd decided earlier that was the place to make a stand if they had to. Cate said it was the most likely point of entry.

"Are you sure you're steady enough for this?" he asked her.

"I'm good. Just follow my lead. Don't fire unless I do. When you shoot, do like I said and aim for the body, not the head or the legs. Shoot to kill, Nick. Safety off?"

He checked it. "Yeah. Cate?"

"What?"

"I do love you."

"Get over there beside that hutch thing. I'll be behind the stove so don't aim in that direction. Cover the back door and windows beside it. I'll take the interior door in case they find another way in and come looking for us."

Nick did as she ordered. He felt secure in the knowledge that his aunt was safely concealed. The entrance to the wine cellar was a sliding panel in the adjacent dining room. Not exactly a secret entrance, but without the lights on in there, it would appear as just another section of the wall.

So, it was just Cate and himself. He heard her speaking on her phone in a low voice. Calling Mercier, informing him backup was needed now. Then she stopped talking and the silence was deafening.

All he could hear was the distant ticking of the ancient grandfather clock in the foyer. Suddenly it bonged twice and he jumped, almost squeezing the trigger.

Okay, he had to get calm here. Like before surgery. This was an operation of sorts. He drew in a deep breath and released it slowly, then another. All the while, he listened.

It occurred to him that he might be able to use what Vinland had set him up to do. He concentrated on the outside, let his mind wander in search of someone out there. He didn't really know what he was doing, he realized, and had almost given up when a strand of thought hit him like a mallet.

How to take her alive? Asleep? Vines up to the window.

"One is climbing up to your bedroom," he whispered to Cate.

She didn't demand to know how he knew that. "Stay put. Let him come to us. Keep your eyes on the outside door. They might approach from two fronts."

Nick thought he'd better add what else he knew. "They want you alive."

She gave a low chuckle. "As if." After a few seconds, she whispered, "How many? Can you tell?"

"Four," he answered without even thinking about it. Then he wondered how he knew that. Was it a guess? "I *think* there are four," he added.

"See what else you can get," she ordered in a gruff whisper.

Nick tried, but his own thoughts were too chaotic to pick up any one thing. Suddenly, he cried, "Don't shoot! Sophia!"

The kitchen door slammed open and a huge figure dashed in, spraying bullets. Nick fired once and the body lurched forward, toppled onto the table and scattered the loaded guns to the floor. More shots rang out from the dining room. A deep voice grunted, cursed in Italian and another shot silenced it.

"Sophia?" Nick called out, knowing she was in there.

"Hold fire," she answered.

Nick met her at the door and helped her over to his

shelter behind the hutch. There were broken dishes from stray bullets and guns all over the floor. "Cate, are you okay?"

She didn't answer.

"Cate?" he called again, hoping she was only deafened by the gunfire and hadn't heard him. "Were you hit?"

"The back door!" Sophia exclaimed, grabbing at his sleeve. "She has gone outside!"

Nick didn't know what to do. He couldn't leave Sophia by herself, but he needed to go after Cate. She had no business out there prowling around with two more men looking for her.

"Go, go!" Sophia demanded. "I will be fine."

"Don't come after us," Nick warned.

"I will stay here or go back to the cellar."

Nick was already halfway out the door when he heard the next shots. Ducking low and running for the front of the house, he almost stumbled over Armando. He automatically dropped to his knees and felt for a carotid pulse. Steady. "Stay down," he warned in case Armando could hear him.

Creeping up to the corner, Nick peered around the edge. Cate was kneeling over a body near the fountain. He watched as she stood, shoulders sagging, head down. Nick ran to her, noting the other body sprawled nearby. He didn't quite trust his count, but she obviously did.

"Take cover, Cate!" he ordered before he reached her.

"We got them all," she replied. "You and Sophia okay?"

"Yes, but Armando's hit. Have you seen Pietro?"

"Dead," she replied, gesturing at the body she had been kneeling over. "Head shot."

Nick glanced around. "The other guy?"

"Over there." She pointed.

"I wonder which one is Adin," Nick said. He wished Mercier had sent a photo or something. "We should see if they have any identification."

They checked the pockets of the two in the yard and found nothing, not so much as a gas receipt. "Not much hope that the ones inside have anything, either," Cate said. "It's pretty much SOP not to carry your wallet when you do something like this."

"Look, lights coming up the road," he said. "Several cars. We'd better get back to the kitchen and reload."

"It's backup," she said, getting to her feet. "Sophia probably called in the locals."

"Let's not take chances. Help me get Armando inside."

An hour later, the bodies were cleared away, and Cate made coffee while Sophia charmed the local constable. He was an older man, but a good twenty years her junior. Nevertheless, Sophia had him wrapped around her little finger.

Nick had commandeered the dining room where Armando was laid out on the grand mahogany table getting emergency treatment for bullet wounds to the thigh and shoulder.

An ambulance screamed in the distance. Cate took in coffee for Nick and a half bottle of Scotch whiskey she'd found for Armando. "Can he have this?" she asked Nick.

"No, the medics are almost here and they'll give him morphine. I'll ride with him to the hospital." Nick took the Scotch from her and swallowed a healthy swig to settle his nerves. Adrenaline was rapidly bleeding out of his system, leaving him a little shaky.

"Okay, you go with him, but I'm going to Florence now, just so you know."

"What! Are you crazy?" He couldn't believe this.

"Psychiatrists aren't supposed to use that term, are they?"

"Only if it fits and it does. Adin might not be among the dead here. What if he's with Vinland?"

She shrugged. "Everybody's got to be somewhere, but why guard somebody who's been immobile for hours?"

"You can't *drive*, Cate," he reminded her.

"Good point. You want to chauffeur me?"

Nick placed the temporary bandage on Armando's leg. "Vinland means that much to you?"

"Jealous?" Cate teased, then relented. "His wife, Dawn, is one of my best friends and so is Eric. He'd do the same for me. If he's hurt, hours could count, Nick. Even using the private jet, the team won't make it there for a while."

"Why haven't they sent the Florence police to find him then?"

"Because the police aren't all that prudent. Their version of SWAT would rush in with guns blazing. Whether he's alone or not, that could get him killed. Besides, we aren't supposed to have agents working over here unless they're authorized, which Eric never is."

"You don't know where to look for him," Nick argued.

"Yeah, I do. I have the coordinates."

"Mercier gave you Vinland's location? What the hell was he thinking?"

"That I'm stuck here, helpless to do anything. I asked, and he probably thought it'd make me feel better, not being totally out of the loop."

"If Vinland's alive, he won't be alone, will he?" Nick asked. But he knew the answer as well as she did. "Adin could be with him. These men were thinking of taking you alive, back to him. Right?"

"Probably." She turned to head upstairs to get her stuff. "So you coming or what?"

The ambulance had reached the house and the sing-song siren had stopped. Nick checked Armando's bandages, satisfied he had stopped the bleeding that had almost killed the man. The bullets would have to come out, but it wasn't as if Nick could do surgery himself even if he were able.

He also knew that if he didn't go with Cate, she would only find another way.

If Vinland was found dead, Cate would need comfort. If he was too injured to move, Nick could provide emergency treatment, just as he'd done with Armando. And if he was immobilized and being guarded, Nick figured he could keep Cate from doing anything drastic until her team arrived. She was definitely against going in with "all guns blazing." She had stated that was why Mercier refused to depend on the police for the rescue.

"All right, we'll go and assess the situation," he said, "but so you know, I feel a decided lack of enthusiasm for this little venture."

"Noted. Let's grab the handguns and a couple of the old automatics. We can't let the constable see us."

Sophia had suggested they stow all the weapons that weren't used in the gun battle in the cellar entrance to take down later. He quietly opened the panel that concealed them and took a couple, handing them off to Cate and adding ammo to his jacket pockets. "I don't think she wants the locals to know she has so much firepower. I imagine some of these pieces are illegal."

"I know so," Cate replied with a grin. "Sophie baby's still a wild child. Can you believe what she did? I think she misses the old days when she fought with the Resistance."

"Obviously. So how do we get out of here and to the car with these? The front yard is crawling with cops and medics."

"They'll be all over Armando when he's taken out to the bus. We'll go out the back, around to the car and pull out behind them. Will you tell Sophia we're going?"

Nick headed into the kitchen, pulled his aunt away from her conversation with the constable and briefly whispered their plan. "She feels she has to do this and I have to be with her."

"Of course you do." Sophia wished them luck and assured him she'd take care of matters on the home front, this investigation into what the constable kept calling a "robbery." No one had disabused him of that notion. "I will have plenty of protection to remain with me." She smiled sweetly at the constable who waited patiently across the room. "You and Cate return here when you are finished, Nicholas. You promise?"

He kissed her powdered cheek and promised. He only hoped they stayed alive to fulfill it.

Chapter 12

Cate didn't like having to bring Nick along, but she hadn't had much choice. She needed a driver. Though she had teased him about it, he had proved he could handle a weapon. That had surprised her right from the get-go. He actually handled himself really well. She had seen new agents who'd done great in training fold up like a lawn chair when facing real-time danger. Nick had nerves of steel in a crisis, even if he was a little shaky afterward. That was to be expected.

Maybe they weren't so different after all. Nick faced fear head-on. He did what he had to do, regardless. She was so proud of him, but she also felt this need to keep him safe when she could. Short of knocking him out, she couldn't figure a way to keep him out of this when they reached their destination.

They had another, more immediate problem. "I'll have to commandeer another car," she told him.

"Why?" he asked.

She smiled when he didn't even bother to protest the theft. "This one doesn't have a GPS. Problem is, the newer vehicles can't be hotwired and the older ones, like this, don't have the systems. I'll need keys."

He drove on. Dawn would soon be breaking and they were on the outskirts of the city. She had to act fast before everybody was up and about. "There," she said, pointing at a new upscale house with fairly good cover around it and no close neighbors. "Stop here."

He pulled over on the side of the road beside the short driveway. "What now?"

"Wait here," she instructed. It was a simple matter to gain entrance. Luck was with her and she found the owner's car keys on a hook just inside the back door. She'd worried she might have to search the place for them or actually hold up the owner to get them. Moments later, she returned. "Let's get the weapons and go." They left the first car where it was, walked back up the driveway and took the other one.

"Everything went slick as a whistle. Good sign," she said, fiddling with the GPS.

Once they were on the road again, he finally commented. "Did they teach auto theft in spy school?"

"I was top of the class. Don't worry, we'll bring it back when we're through. Or Mercier will make it right."

"You got that thing working?"

"I do. I punched in the coordinates and it looks like it's

not far. Go right at the next exit. It's is a warehouse/storage building on the outskirts, this side of the city. Mercier had an aerial view and told me what it was. The trick might be finding the right structure. He only mentioned the basic coordinates, 43 latitude and 11 longitude. Let's hope it's not one of many."

Nick followed the directions she read off the GPS system and they were soon in an area of Florence no tourists ever saw. Up close, Cate saw that it looked like any old, little-used warehouse area in any large city around the world. There were five buildings grouped together that looked pretty much the same. They backed up against the Amo River and fronted a common packed-dirt area large enough for trucks to load and unload. Large copses of trash trees served as barriers on either side of the grouping, separating the eyesores from newer businesses up and down the road.

"Pull over by the trees," she said. "I'd better continue on foot."

"You're not leaving me here," Nick told her in no uncertain terms.

"Okay, but you follow my lead. Do just what I tell you and don't argue."

He nodded, parked, got out of the car and retrieved the automatics from the backseat, handing her one. "Any idea where to start?"

She walked down the side of the road for some fifty yards, then pointed at the middle structure. "That one." She had spied the broken padlock on the side door.

He followed her as she crept around to the back, hoping

for an open loading bay on the river side. No such luck. There was a metal stairway leading up to a door at the top. Likely the offices were up there, leaving room downstairs for cargo.

"Back to the side door," she said, moving around Nick to take the lead.

"There are no vehicles outside," he noted. "Maybe that means Vinland is alone in there."

"Or not," Cate replied wryly. "Let's assume not."

"Okay. Let's assume that if you open that door, we could get a face full of lead."

She chuckled. "That did occur to me. So stand back and squat down. These walls probably aren't thick enough to stop bullets." Following her own instructions, she crouched down on one side of the door, reached up and opened the door a crack.

Nothing happened. Didn't mean it wouldn't. Still to one side, she gave the door a shove that opened it fully. It banged against the inside wall.

Still no sound from inside. "I'm going in," she said.

"Me first," Nick declared and beat her to the punch. He ducked and rolled. Cate followed, grabbing him by one arm and urging him behind a large wooden crate.

It was dark inside, but not totally. Weak light from the upstairs windows, front and back, and the open door behind them threw eerie shadows over dust-covered crates and boxes.

Cate sniffed. No smell of death. If Eric's body had been left here, she would know it by now. Maybe they had the wrong warehouse, but she didn't think so. There were subtle signs of recent activity. She could see the dust on the floor had been disturbed beyond what she and Nick had caused.

"Tracks lead up the stairs," he whispered as if he was tuned in on her thoughts. Probably was.

"See if you can sense him," she said quietly.

He closed his eyes for a few seconds, then shook his head. Even as he did that, she heard his grunt of surprise, followed by an urgent whisper. "He's waiting!"

Cate didn't have to ask who. It wouldn't be Eric, or Nick would be going to him. He had obviously stumbled on Adin's thoughts while trolling for Eric's. "Where? Can you tell?"

He gestured upstairs with his pistol. Cate couldn't help but note how determined and confident Nick looked in that position, assault weapon slung over one shoulder, palming that pistol like he was born with it in his hand. He was actually eager to charge up there, she thought, but was doing exactly as he had promised. Waiting for her orders.

Cate wished to hell she knew what to do. If only she could read Adin's mind and get a handle on what he had planned. Had he killed Eric? She wondered if Nick could...

"He's not dead. Adin wanted you to see him do it," Nick said in a low voice. "He knew you would come, but he thought you'd be a prisoner of the ones he sent to get you. He knows we're here and he's wondering what you'll do next."

"Eric's alive? You're sure?"

"Adin left him that way, but I'm not getting anything

from Vinland. He's here, though." He continued to watch the upper floor as he spoke. "Up there somewhere."

Cate was at a loss. If they waited for the team to get here and Adin was surrounded with no hope of escape, he'd kill Eric for sure.

Nick grasped her forearm as if he were afraid she'd do something stupid. He leaned close, his mouth near her ear. "He knows there are two of us. He's planning his escape out the back and down the river. Boat's waiting." Nick paused as if to listen, then continued. "Door's unlocked and ready. Now he's waiting, though, hoping you'll come up."

"Can he see us?"

"He did, but now he's trying to decide what to do about Vinland. Should he go the length of the building to finish him off or stay near the back door? Distract him. Talk to him. I'm going up there through the back door," Nick declared.

"No! Nick, you can't!" Fear crashed through her.

But Nick was already headed for the open door, on hands and knees in the shadows. "Keep him busy, Cate!" he rasped. And then he was gone.

"Adin! You looking for me?" Cate shouted. "Too chicken to come and get me?"

She heard a sound from above, footsteps, a door opening. God, she hoped it wasn't that back door. He'd meet Nick coming up those outside stairs.

"You want revenge so bad, come take it, you cowardly sonofabitch! Sending your sister to do your work for you. What kind of a man are you anyway?" Taunting him seemed the best way to keep him off balance. Besides, it felt great to yell at the bastard. "It's your fault she's dead!"

"Damn you, Yankee bitch! You killed her and I will kill you!"

"Big talk for such a little man," she yelled. "A girly-man, we call your kind. Only that's an insult to girls! Your sister had more guts than you. C'mon, pipsqueak, die for your bloody cause. Get your three dozen virgins, like you'd know what to do with one!"

Adin rushed out on the landing and fired a barrage across the box she hid behind. Cate ducked down in a ball, curling over her weapon. She was afraid to fire up there in case Nick had already made it inside. And Eric was up there somewhere. Instead, she stuck her automatic around the edge of the box and fired at the wall, well below the landing.

He returned fire, hitting the barrel of her weapon. The blow vibrated all the way up to her shoulder, dislodging her grip. She quickly drew her pistol, crawled to the opposite side of the box and fired three shots. He needed to believe Nick was still in here with her. "That the best you got, hotshot?" she yelled.

Again he fired, but the volley was brief. "Hey, you ready to give up now? Your aim's lousy. Out of ammo yet?" she taunted.

"He's dead," Nick called down.

Cate scrambled from behind her cover and dashed for the stairs. The suddenness of her move made her a little dizzy, but she kept her balance, grabbed on to the iron railing and made pretty good time halfway up.

Nick met her and hauled her into his arms. He squeezed her so tight, she couldn't move. Then he kissed her, destroying what was left of her equilibrium. When he finally released her mouth, he looked down at her in the dim light.

"You weren't hit, were you?" he asked, running his hands over her arms, up to her shoulders and down her back.

"No, I'm okay."

"Thank God!" He kissed her again, then cradled her head against his shoulder as if they had all the time in the world to make out on the stairs. She wished they had, but this wasn't over yet.

"We have to find Eric," she reminded him.

"Start at the far end down there," Nick told her, leading the way, still holding one of her arms.

"Did you check Adin? You sure he's dead?" Cate glanced back at the body, but the lighting was so poor she could barely see it.

"I am a doctor, remember? I know what a person can't live without. Heads count."

"I told you to aim for the body, the biggest target!"

He sighed and tightened the arm he had around her shoulders. "I *was* aiming for the body."

Cate realized she was too used to working with partners who were expert marksmen. Nick had gone too far beyond the call of duty to suffer any critique of his skills. "You did just fine, Nicky. I'm so sorry you had to do this. I really am."

"Yeah. Me, too, but I'd do it again. No regrets. I think

Vinland's in here," he said, opening the door to the office nearest the front of the building.

Cate stumbled forward when she saw the form in the corner curled in a fetal position.

Nick was already there, checking for a pulse at Eric's neck. "Weak," he reported. "Help me untie him."

Cate pulled and tugged at the bonds and they soon had him free. He hadn't moved.

"Drugged to oblivion and probably dehydrated," Nick grunted. "We have to get him to a hospital quick. Help me get him up. I'll carry him to the car."

"Water!" Cate said. "We have to get some liquids in him."

"He's in no shape to drink. He'll need an IV. Let's go." Together they managed to get Eric down the stairs and to the vehicle where Nick dumped him into the backseat. "Get in with him. Try to wake him up."

She quickly positioned Eric's head in her lap and tried repeatedly to rouse a response from him.

Nick had changed, Cate thought. Not once after they'd arrived in Florence had he urged caution. She still could hardly believe he had come with her without protesting all the way. And during their confrontation with Adin, he had seemed to discard all his doubts about what she could and couldn't do.

Maybe she had proved to him that she could handle herself in a dangerous field op. Odd that her part in all this had proved just the opposite to her. Everything had turned out well, thank God, but throughout the confrontation with Adin, she had truly felt her limitations. She had managed, but only just. Maybe it had taken this last self-directed mission to convince her it was time to step down. It hurt like hell to admit that, but now she knew and accepted what had to be.

As Nick drove like a maniac through the early-morning traffic, she continued trying to wake Eric, but he never stirred. This brought home to her just how tenuous life could be for an agent doing what they did, no matter how well they did it.

Eric was the best. He had all the gifts necessary from his well-controlled psychic ability to his expertise in the martial arts. How could he have been taken? This, together with her own recent near-death experience, sure blew holes in her fantasy that she was invulnerable.

When they arrived at the hospital, Eric was still unconscious. But mostly thanks to Nick, he was also still alive.

"Well, you did it," Nick told her once they had turned Eric over to the emergency staff. "You saved your friend."

"*We* did it," she replied. "I need to call in. Eric's wife, Dawn, must be frantic."

"Take a minute," he advised. "Catch your breath."

She reached up and palmed the side of his face, feeling the stubble of his beard, noting how disreputable he looked. How different this man was from the carefully groomed, ultra clean-cut physician. "You sort of worked up a sweat, too, doc. How're you doing?"

"Crashing," he admitted, running a hand through his dusty hair. "That sudden letdown when the adrenaline quits pumping."

"Tell me about it," she said with a short laugh. "It's become a way of life I'm about ready to chuck."

He stilled suddenly, his hand still on his head. "Seriously?"

Cate just smiled. She trailed her hand down from his face to his chest and gave it a pat. "I really have to make that call. The team should be landing soon."

The team consisted of Vanessa Senate and Danielle Michaels from COMPASS and Jack Mercier himself. Dawn, a crackerjack agent with the National Security Agency, had been allowed to join them. They arrived in force, hurrying down the hallway where Nick and Cate stood waiting.

"Where is he?" Dawn demanded. "*How* is he?"

Cate put a hand on her shoulder. "He'll be fine, Dawn. They're pumping him full of liquids to rehydrate him. Soon as he gets the drugs out of his system, he'll come around." She pointed. "He's in ICU. You have clearance to go on in."

Nick gestured to a small waiting room used only for private consultations. "I asked if we could use this so we won't be interrupted."

"Thanks, Sandro, that was thoughtful," Mercier said. They all went in and when they were seated, Mercier leaned forward, his hands clasped between his knees. "How did they take Eric, do you know yet?"

Cate sighed. "Taser. They found the marks." She gave Jack the full account of all that had happened at the villa and then at the warehouse.

Nick covered one of her hands with his and muttered,

"Don't forget about the car, Cate. That will need to be returned."

Cate recounted that, as well. "How do you think they found us, Jack?"

"Eric had been snooping around Florence, trying to locate Adin. One of his hired guns slipped a tracker on Eric's vehicle to keep up with him, see where he went. Unfortunately, he followed you from the hospital that night. Made sense you'd be in some isolated place and that area fit the bill. Adin sent a little task force after you."

"At least we were ready for them."

"You've done a good job, Cate," Jack told her. "It looks as if you've surpassed everybody's hopes. We'll have to wait a few years, make certain the heat's off, and maybe you can come back to the field."

"We've missed you," Vanessa said with a grin.

"Eric might not have made it if you hadn't jumped the gun," Dani chimed in. "And you, too, Dr. Sandro. I wonder if you didn't miss your calling!"

Cate turned her hand so that hers grasped Nick's. She swallowed hard. "My reflexes are too slow and my vision's not improving. I did all I could because I had to, but if it hadn't been for Nick, Eric would be dead and so would I. Any partner working with me on an op would have double the risk, so it's time for me to step down. I want the relocation you offered, Jack."

Dead silence met her announcement. Then they all started talking at once, everyone protesting her decision but Nick. He just looked at her with a sadness deeper than she had ever seen in his expression.

She would have to leave everything behind, but none of it mattered except Nick. Knowing she'd never be able to see him again was the worst. She loved him, always had, always would, but he couldn't come with her and she couldn't stay. A tear rolled down her cheek and she brushed it away, impatient with herself and her damned emotions. They just wouldn't stay below the surface where they belonged.

"We'll see about that *later,*" Mercier said with a tone of finality that meant the subject was closed for now.

"I'll be fine," she assured Nick, forcing a smile.

Hours passed. Nick sorely needed to get Cate alone and talk about this decision of hers. They needed to figure out some other way to ensure her safety from anyone still hoping to fulfill that contract Adin had put on her. He was dead, sure, but he probably had dozens of relatives who would take up the cause. But Cate wouldn't budge from the waiting room and neither would the other agents.

Mercier disappeared a time or two, but always returned within minutes. They talked business, but only in general terms. They caught Cate up on their family news. They avoided the topic of Cate quitting and relocating, definitely the elephant in the room. It was all Nick could think about.

Cate had either found a way of keeping him out of her thoughts or his were too chaotic to connect with hers.

Finally, Dawn emerged from Vinland's room and joined them, all smiles. "He's awake! Still shaky and way too talkative."

"God, that's such good news, Dawn. When can he go home?" Vanessa asked.

"I don't know yet. He's still pretty weak."

Mercier called and made reservations for all of them at the closest hotel so they could get some rest and reconvene later at the hospital. He and his crew were jetlagged and hadn't had much sleep in the past twenty-four hours. Cate and Nick were physically and mentally exhausted to say the least.

Cate didn't suggest that they share a room, but accompanied him to his once they got there. Nick was so relieved. As soon as the door closed, he turned to her and took her in his arms. "Cate, think about this decision of yours. I know I argued for it when Vinland first suggested it, but—"

She put her fingers over his lips, then replaced them with her mouth. The kiss burned away thought entirely as their bodies pressed together with a vengeance. He backed her to the nearest bed, pushed her onto it and followed her down. Clothes flew this way and that.

"I need you," Cate gasped against his mouth. "I need you *now!*"

Nick rolled her beneath him and pushed inside her without hesitation. She was so ready and he couldn't wait another second. Fast and furiously, he took her, a hope at the back of his mind that this would change hers, make her see how desperately he wanted her, needed her, and how much time they had wasted fighting this very thing.

"I can't let you go." He ground out the words, teeth clenched and lungs heaving with the effort to make her see, make her know, make her feel...

Her wordless cry caught him by surprise, interrupting his concentration on giving her pleasure. Nick lost it completely and abandoned all control. He poured himself into her and cried out himself, an animal sound that reverberated right down to his soul. They lay together, boneless and exhausted. Replete and satisfied, but yet not quite that. Cate was planning to go soon, where he would never find her.

He wanted so much to hold her gently, run his hands over that delicious body, tell her of all the feelings he had hidden, even from himself, for so long. He loved Cate, so deeply that it had scared him into denying it. Scared her, too, he figured. Both of them were so damned independent, they had fought becoming half of the one they should have become years ago.

By the time he had the right words formed, her breathing had slowed and her eyes were closed. They had not slept at all yesterday, last night or today. Nick couldn't bring himself to wake her. But it was only midafternoon, he thought. Before they went to dinner this evening, they would settle things. They would find a way, he decided as he drifted off to sleep beside her.

When he woke up at seven that evening, Cate was gone.

Chapter 13

"Cate, it doesn't have to be forever," Danielle murmured as they settled in the limo that would take them to the airport.

"It will be," Cate replied. "He would never forgive my leaving him like that, without so much as a goodbye, see you later."

"At least you had today. And your time together at that villa," Dani reminded her. "Is there anything I can do to help?"

Cate shook her head and leaned it against the tinted window. "I just need to get this over with, leave Italy behind me and forget about it." As if she ever could.

"It's not just Italy, remember," Dani said. "What about your family? Did you call them?"

"No."

"This is hard, I know, but faking your death is the best solution for everybody. Adin's death will cause a big stir everywhere and you'll get the credit for taking him out."

"And then I die. That way, none of his cronies will be after Nick for it and I'll be safely dead. You going to my funeral? Don't send carnations. I hate 'em," Cate said, trying to inject a note of humor. It fell flat.

"Don't worry, you won't be remembered," Jack assured her. "Your demise will make a very high-profile splash in the papers. We're initiating charges against your reporter buddy, Jakes, under the Intel Identities Protection Act. Going for the max, fifty-thousand fine or ten years in stir—both if we can get it."

"That should keep his mouth shut for a while. But I hate what this will do to your parents and your brother," Vanessa said. She was all about family and had one the size of Texas.

"It seems cruel," Cate agreed, "but they'll get over it pretty quickly. They never quite knew what to do with me anyway. That's why they kept trying for years to palm me off on Nick. I was a lot of trouble, I guess."

"I bet!" Danielle said with a snort. "You're a terrible tease and the worst daredevil I know. I can imagine what they must have gone through, poor people."

Cate sighed. "I love 'em, though. And I do hate to leave you guys. Never had such good friends. Like minds and all that."

Dani patted her arm. "You'll make more where you're going."

"Wonder where that will be," Cate said. Not that she

really cared. Depression had set in and she just wasn't ready to battle it yet.

The others gave her hugs and went to the exit where they would board the private jet for D.C.

Mercier stood with Cate, watching them go, waiting for her to start with the questions.

She didn't ask a thing. He would tell her soon enough.

"How does Boise, Idaho sound?" he asked finally.

"Like you might be kidding," Cate replied. Maybe it did matter, after all.

He grinned. "You'll love it."

She gave a wry chuckle. "Okay, so who am I?"

"Elizabeth Anderson. You'll be working in a rehabilitation center, a great way for you to keep up with your exercises and get help with any residual problems you might have from your injury. You'll also be running physical security on the house. The pay's okay, not what you were making, but it's the best I could do on short notice."

"That's fine. Thanks, Jack," she said without even bothering to pretend any enthusiasm.

"You're welcome…Elizabeth. Here are your papers and your ticket to Boise."

"Just call me Liz," she said, accepting the fake identification he handed her. She thumbed through the envelope. Passport, Idaho driver's license, social security card, letters of recommendation, plane ticket and a stack of U.S. bills to tide her over.

It wasn't the comedown she had expected. But God, she felt so alone already. Jack gave her a perfunctory hug and stepped back. He tapped the envelope she held. "Feel free to change that if you want anonymity, even from me. Remember all the tricks?"

"Of course, but thanks for saving me the trouble."

He smiled encouragement. "Good luck, Cate. As of now, I guess you're on your own." He added, almost as if he couldn't help himself, "But if you're ever in *real* trouble, call my private number and I'll help if I can. Unofficially, you understand?"

"Got it. Thanks again, Jack, for everything." They shook hands and he left, following his agents to their flight. Keeping with their tradition of heading out on a mission without a goodbye, neither said the word. Better to assume you'd turn up alive to continue right where you left off. This parting was final, though. She'd never see any of them again. "Goodbye," she whispered when he was out of sight.

Cate had already decided she would make the break complete. She'd live on her own terms, choose her own name and her own destination. It was a matter of control. She was taking charge of her own life.

She exchanged her ticket, went to two other counters and purchased others as a smoke screen. There would be other stops and different modes of travel, some that didn't leave a paper trail in any name.

Next, she made a call to two banks in McLean and transferred all her assets into a numbered account in Lucerne. Jack might trace her funds there if he cared to try, but no one without his official pull could ever get the information.

That only left the tracking gizmo under the skin of her

shoulder. She went straight to the gift shop, intent on finding something with a keenly sharp edge and a packet of large Band-Aids. The pain of removing her last little link with COMPASS would be nothing compared to the agony of cutting Nick out of her life, but maybe it would distract her.

When she had completed the simple surgery, Cate emerged from the ladies' room. She surreptitiously dropped the tracker in the open tote bag of a passing stranger headed for the opposite end of the terminal.

After she boarded the plane, Cate couldn't keep her mind off Nick. He would still be sleeping. Sneaking out of that bed and that room had been the hardest thing she'd ever done. She had ached to touch him all over, to kiss him with all the strength and passion she had and make love with him until they couldn't.

This was *your* choice, she reminded herself sternly. She could have stayed. But how many close calls with death had he suffered this past week just because of her? Staying with him would have kept Nick squarely in the path of anyone who might come after her on Adin's behalf.

Nick hurried to the hospital, betting big on finding Cate there with her friends. But when he arrived, the regular waiting room was full of strangers and the small one where they had met earlier in the day was empty.

Maybe they were all in visiting with Vinland. He asked at the desk, but the nurse looked confused. "We don't have a Vinland listed. Maybe he has been moved to another floor." She checked the computer and shook her head. "No, we have no patient with that name. He is American, you say?"

Nick didn't bother to answer her. He rushed down to the admitting office and asked there whether Vinland had been released. No record of him there, either. Same with the billing office. Surely the U.S. Government was responsible for covering his hospitalization. Insurance left a paper trail a mile long, especially in a place that had socialized medicine. Not this time.

Then he remembered that Cate had handled the admitting. She might have used one of Vinland's aliases. Either that, or Vinland's presence had been deliberately erased. Mercier, again.

Back at the hotel, he got similar answers. The elderly clerk assured him there were no Americans staying at the hotel but him. And yes, his bill had been paid for at check-in time as required. His passport would be returned to him when he checked out. Nick demanded to see it. He hadn't had his passport with him. The clerk handed it over. It was his. Apparently, someone had retrieved it from his apartment.

"Are you leaving now, sir? I will need your key."

Nick handed it over, went straight to the lounge and ordered a double Scotch. Cate was gone. He sipped the drink and looked at his watch. She could be anywhere in the world right now. Mercier would make it impossible to find her.

He closed his eyes and tried his best to connect with her mentally, but he had nothing to focus on, no way to get there, wherever she was.

Maybe she was asleep, her thoughts shut down. Or more likely, he'd dreamed that bunk about mind reading anyway. Probably some post-hypnotic suggestion Vinland had planted in his brain to boost confidence in his already existing powers of observation.

He took another swallow of Scotch, leveled an intense gaze across the bar and tried it on the bartender. Nothing but an inner humming of the godawful elevator music piped into the bar, which could very well be his own brain cells reacting. Not even a recipe for a drink came through.

Hell with it. Nick wanted to get roaring drunk. He'd never allowed himself to do that, never really had the inclination until now. He swallowed the rest of his drink and ordered another. After the third, he decided alcoholism wasn't the best solution to his problems.

He called a cab and went to his apartment. There he'd be alone with the scent of Cate on his guest room pillows and the memory of finding that body at the foot of the stairwell.

He couldn't stay in Florence.

Tomorrow, he'd have to return to the villa and Sophia as he had promised. Maybe he'd stay awhile. His parents were coming to Italy soon and he had promised his aunt a surprise reunion with them.

He should come back to Florence after that and finish monitoring those classes. Then there was the fellowship a little over two months from now. His new *career.*

None of it made any sense to him now. All he wanted to do was find Cate, an impossible quest.

She knew his plans, though. Surely she would find a way to contact him, if only to let him know she was settled and okay with her life. He would never feel settled again.

* * *

The next morning, Nick rented a car and headed back to the villa as planned. He had the awful task of explaining Cate's disappearance to Aunt Sophia.

When he arrived at midday, he found her weeping in the library. "What's wrong?" he asked, putting his arms around her frail little frame. She must be mourning Pietro, of course. And maybe Armando, too, if he hadn't made it.

She raised red-rimmed eyes and sniffed. "Nicholas, please sit down. This will be terribly hard for you to hear."

"What? What is it?"

"Your friend, Mr. Vinland. He phoned thinking you would be here earlier this morning." She cleared her throat and sniffed again, dabbing her eyes with a wet, lace-trimmed handkerchief. "Your Caterina's plane has crashed, Nicholas." She sobbed. "There were no survivors."

Nick's heart nearly stopped. Then he reassured himself. Vinland had suggested they fake Cate's death to keep her safe. This was how they'd done it.

His breath rushed out with relief. Vinland's calling himself must be a subtle message to Nick. He should tell Sophia what was going on, save her some tears. But he remembered that no one was to know. No one, not even her family.

"Mr. Vinland said he and the other people she worked with flew home on their company plane, but apparently Cate elected to take a flight to Denmark. Her parents and brother are there."

Nick felt a niggle of apprehension. Cate had made love

to him by way of a last farewell. Wouldn't she want to have one last look at her family before losing them forever? Had she taken a separate plane? Was the crash real?

"It is noon, let's see if there's anything on the news about it." Sophia moved to the television, a virtual antique set that had seen little use during the time he'd spent here. She turned it on now and found a news channel.

They waited, attention glued to the newscaster as he began relating the disasters of the day.

"A DC-10 Loftair bound for Copenhagen went down less than an hour into its flight from Florence. All fifty-one passengers and crew were lost. Wreckage lies scattered over a mountainous region of Germany near Kassel…"

Nick cut off the television. "She's not *dead*," he said to himself. "She's not."

"Nicholas," his aunt said, taking hold of his arm. "I am so, so sorry you have lost her."

He patted the hands clutched around his forearm. "So am I, Aunt Sophia. So am I."

Nicholas had to know. He had to find Vinland or Mercier and get the truth of *how* he had lost Cate. Was she still alive? Had Mercier set her up with a new identity, never again to be seen by anyone who knew her, or had she really gone down with that plane?

He tried not to think how coincidental it was that a plane headed for the city where her parents were staying had crashed only hours after she had disappeared. No government agency would crash a plane full of people just to fake the death of an operative. The crash had definitely happened. Aerial views of it had been posted on the newscast. Nick felt sick.

It took an hour and two glasses of wine to convince Sophia he was stable enough to be left alone. He had just persuaded her to go to her room and lie down when his cell phone rang.

It was his mother, her voice thick with tears. "We just heard from the Olins, Nick. They were notified Cate was killed in a plane crash."

"Yes, Mom, I heard. How are they holding up?"

"Not well. Your dad and I are on our way to Copenhagen now to be with them. I expect we'll travel back to the States with them, too, after...after Cate's been..."

"After the body's recovered," Nick said finishing her sentence for her, his voice stiff and foreign, even to his own ears. He couldn't bring himself to say *her* body. He couldn't believe she was dead. He didn't believe it. "I'll call you tomorrow, Mom. My condolences to the Olins."

"That sounds cold," his mother admonished. "Nick, are you all right?"

"I need to go, Mom. I'll be at the crash site for the next few days assisting with the recovery. I'll call you." He hung up before she could respond. The Olins were in good hands.

He was going to Germany. He had to know.

Chapter 14

A full ten days of sorting body parts and charred remains left Nick numb with despair. No one wanted that job. When he'd shown up volunteering, the German authorities readily accepted his help in the makeshift morgue. Now it was over and all passengers and crew had been accounted for except two who had seats nearest the engine that had exploded. Was Cate one of them?

Her name was not on the passenger list. He learned from her dad that Mercier had notified them that she was on the plane. She would have traveled under an alias considering that there could still be assassins out there looking for her, expecting to be paid if they fulfilled that contract. Maybe they had found her. The explosion was still under investigation. It could have been a bomb. But

Cate had left in such a rush, when would anyone have had time to plant one?

His mind ran in circles, one moment worrying that he had missed identifying her remains, the next clinging to the surety that she was still alive. She had to be.

He took his leave when they declared it was over and flew home.

"You missed the memorial service," his mother said, one of the first sentences out of her mouth when he arrived.

She's not dead! he wanted to shout, but he didn't. If she were still alive, no one was supposed to know. So he apologized to his parents, visited hers and gave his condolences in person. They were sad, but seemed to be getting on with their lives in short order, doting on their son, planning his future. Nick resented that so much, he had to get away from them in a hurry before he said something cruel.

Maybe it took this for him to realize how much Cate had needed him when they were young. Back then, it really had been him and her against the world. No wonder his own parents had pushed him so hard to look after Cate. They probably saw how wrapped up in their son Cate's parents were at the time and felt sorry for her. He did, too, now.

Next mission was to find Mercier or Vinland and wring the truth out of them. A nod was all he needed from one of them. Was she still alive? He would promise not to try to find her if they would only give him that much.

The search led him nowhere. COMPASS and SEXTANT truly were covert teams. No one would give him an office address. He prowled D.C. and McLean, hoping by chance to spot one of the agents he had met. Too much ground to cover.

Exhausted by his efforts to find Cate, Nick almost accepted that he had failed. Still, he held on to a shred of hope.

He began the psychiatry fellowship in Baltimore when the time came and immersed himself in work. Months later, he qualified in his new specialty, but felt no satisfaction in it. He continued his search.

It dawned on Nick that he was caught in the grip of true obsession. This had gone on too long, but he couldn't give it up. He couldn't mourn Cate. He simply did not believe she was dead.

Denial. Common sense said he was stuck in that first stage of grief. He denied that, too. One important stage of qualifying as a psychiatrist was undergoing psychiatric evaluation himself.

He successfully faked his way through that, but knew in his heart he was not ready to set up a practice and work with patients until he got his own head straight.

"Catie, Catie, where are you now?" he asked, desperate and dejected, his hopes fading as he stood gazing at nothing out the window of his apartment near the hospital.

Boston.

Nick blinked and his breath caught. The faint single word that blipped through his mind shocked him to immobility.

"Where?" he demanded. Nothing. No answer. Had he imagined it? Maybe so, but he felt powerless to ignore it. He turned, snatched up the phone and made reservations on the next hop available. He grabbed his wallet, threw some clothes into his weekender and headed out the door.

* * *

Cate could have kicked herself. What had she done? For months, she had kept up that shield, only allowing herself an occasional check on Nick to make sure he was okay. But this time she had caught him at a particularly bad moment. He had seemed so lost, actually calling to her. She had slipped. Just for a second, her need to touch him in any way she could had overpowered her and she'd actually answered.

He would come here to Boston. She would have to block him out permanently or he would find her. How dangerous would that be after all this time? Months had passed. Everyone believed she was dead, but Nick and Mercier, and she knew that even Mercier couldn't be sure.

Cate had bought a ticket for the Copenhagen flight, a believable misdirection since her parents were there. Mercier had used the coincidental crash to establish her death instead of his original plan. He would have considered that more palatable to her parents than telling them she took a bullet during the confrontation with Adin. She'd had three tickets that day. Mercier couldn't have known which plane she was really on.

Nick had been ready to accept her death. Why hadn't she let him? She almost regretted that her sixth sense had come back. It had returned gradually, letting her grasp an occasional thought. Lately it had become more reliable.

Cate went back to work, putting her class through their paces, teaching them to defend themselves. They were hiding here at Safe Haven from bullying husbands and significant others.

Cate had come to realize that she didn't have to risk her

neck every day in order to make a difference in the world. She made a difference here, adjusting attitudes, creating self-confidence, turning doormats into steel doors. She was stronger than ever herself, no longer needing the parental attention she had vied so hard to get. She'd had love all along. Nick's.

That knowledge alone was a consolation, but so was her work. No one left here unprepared to deal with what came next for them, whether it was facing their attackers in court or setting up a new life somewhere they couldn't be found. She was good at that last option, too.

Sometimes they let themselves be found like she had almost done. In a way, she understood why they would do it and—though her circumstances weren't the same as theirs—why she had done it. Hope that love could change things. Usually it didn't, unfortunately.

When she had finished for the day, Cate showered and curled up in her room with a book. But she couldn't concentrate on the page. Her thoughts kept returning to Nick and how he had refused for so long to let go of her. He couldn't have gone on the way he was.

If she were honest, that had not been a real slip of the mind, giving him that information. She loved him so much, she couldn't bear to know he suffered. At least now he would know she was alive and maybe he could get on with his life.

Nick somehow knew he'd get no more clues about where to find Cate. He didn't even know where that one had come from, but he was so revved. She *was* alive.

On the short flight to Boston, he spent the time trying to figure out what she would be doing. Nothing to do with law enforcement. What did that leave? What unrelated skills did she possess?

When he landed, he went to the car rental desk and got a vehicle, then headed downtown to get a hotel room. There, he grabbed a phone book and began to scan the *Yellow Pages, A* to *Z,* hoping to get some ideas about where she might work.

He knew Cate better than anyone else. What would she agree to do? She'd have to be the best at whatever that was. Something physical was the best bet.

He grabbed the small writing tablet and pen provided by the hotel and began his list of potential occupations with *Bouncer.* Maybe she'd be good at that, but it would be too public. He crossed it off and ran his finger down the page of businesses listed.

This would take a while, he realized, so he stopped and ordered room service with plenty of coffee. Hours later, he was still at it, but finally took a break when his eyes began to burn. He slept, then picked up where he'd left off.

When he reached the *M*'s and hit martial arts, something clicked. He remembered Cate doing stretching exercises, including that slow, graceful progression of moves taught in karate. Almost like a dance. Her balance had improved with that, he recalled. It was somewhere to start anyway.

He continued his search of the phone book until morning when he could get out there and check all the martial arts schools in Boston. God, they were everywhere!

Three days later, he had narrowed the field considerably. He had figured her most prudent choice would be to teach children or women. Contact with a lot of males might cause those students to discuss their remarkable, very attractive, tall, blond instructor with other men they knew. As a man, he certainly would. That could lead to discovery, which she would want to avoid.

On the pretext of having a sister who was terrified of men, he inquired everywhere about classes with a female who was really capable. That led to several interesting interviews, but no Cate.

Then he lucked out. One owner with no women employed, asked Nick if the sister who needed training was being abused. Nick hung his head, nodding. "And you're a doctor? Got some I.D.?"

Nick showed him. "You know someone who could help her?"

The man hesitated. "Yeah, maybe. A friend of mine mentioned there's this shelter for women. They teach defense, I think. Don't know exactly where it is, though. It's called Safe Haven. Have your sister call. I doubt they'd give a man their address."

Nick thanked him profusely. What a perfect fit that would be for Cate. Double the protection and a job suited to her, using her talents and putting no one at risk if her reaction time faltered or her vision blurred a little.

His excitement dimmed when he realized he'd have the devil of a time finding the place. There had to be a way.

Cate left the Center and headed for her apartment. It had been over a week, ten days actually, since she had checked on Nick and how he was thinking. To tell the truth, she'd been afraid she would cave and let him know where she was.

She hoped he'd had time to settle down, accept the fact that she was alive and get his spirits up again. Not knowing had been his real problem. Now he knew. Maybe she should see.

"Hi, Catie. How's it going?"

She yelped and jumped, nearly losing her balance. He caught her arm, his hand closing around it as if he thought she might run. "Nick! How…how'd you find me?"

"Don't worry. Nobody ratted and I doubt there's an assassin alive who'd go to all this trouble for any amount of money."

Cate disagreed, but she was too glad to see him to argue. She wrapped her arms around his waist and hugged him hard. He held her, but she felt his reluctance. Mad, she thought.

"No, not mad, but I came way too close to madness," he said, a sting in his words. "Do you know how—"

"Yes, I know," she said, burying her face in his neck. "I know all too well. You can't imagine how I've missed you, wished a million times I could call you, meet you somewhere, let you know."

"Did you? Was that you who whispered Boston in my brain or did ol' Vinland have a change of heart?"

"He thinks I'm dead," she said quickly. "They all do, except maybe Jack." She sighed into his collar and inhaled the scent of him, loving the familiar smell and feel.

"Should we be standing out here in the open?" he asked.

"My place is close by," she said, releasing him. "Come on." She took his hand and led the way. She had rented a large garage apartment in the back of an enormous house that backed onto the alley one street over. She could walk to work without being seen and didn't even need a car.

Safe Haven was located in an upscale neighborhood, the eight-bedroom house donated by a wealthy victim who survived her spouse and was left with his fortune.

She hurried up the stairs and unlocked her door after carefully checking for tampering with the lock. Cate drew her .38, entered first and did a thorough, ritual scan of the place, though her alarm system was top flight. "Come on in," she said, tucking the small pistol away in her shoulder bag.

"You do that every time?" he asked, frowning. "What sort of existence have you got here?"

"Standard procedure," she replied. "You're so angry with me, aren't you?"

A range of emotions flashed across his face. "Found you and don't know what to do with you," he admitted, turning away and throwing up his hands.

Cate felt powerless to put him at ease. Sex popped to mind, but she didn't dare suggest it. That was how she'd left him and he didn't need a reminder of that.

"Look, I did it for you, Nick. If I'd stayed, I might have gotten you killed. God knows, I put you in enough danger when we were together. You had to shoot people, get shot at, do things that went against your very nature. I knew you would stick by me, that you'd die to protect me no matter what. That's what I was afraid of."

He faced her again. "You're alive. That's all that matters now."

She shrugged, rubbing her upper arms with her hands. "So where do we go from here? You're satisfied I'm alive and that's it?"

"Hell, no, that's not *it!* What do you think, that I spent all these months looking for you just to say hello?" He stopped. "I don't know what you're thinking. Why don't I know? Why can't I tell?"

She smiled. "Because I don't want you to, Nick. But I'm reading you fairly well. You're mad as hell whether you admit it or not. You're wondering how the devil I could have just up and left you lying there sleeping without so much as a goodbye kiss! You want to hit me for putting you through hell, but you won't because you're a civilized man with great impulse control."

"You missed something, Cate!" he shouted, turning away from her again, hands fisted at his sides. "You missed *why* I feel angry. You missed how much I love you."

Cate risked approaching him from behind and slipped her arms around his waist. "No. I didn't miss that, Nicky," she said quietly. "Sometimes I took it for granted, but I know that's always been there."

He loosened her arms and turned in them, grasping her face in his hands. He kissed her. Finally! Passionately! Cate abandoned herself to whatever happened next. Anything he wanted from now on was his if she had it to give.

"You, Cate," he said vehemently as he broke the kiss. "I want *you.*"

He had her. Man, did he ever. She pushed his jacket off

his shoulders and tore at the buttons on his shirt. He reached for the edge of her sweater and tugged it over her head. The sports bra followed it, sailing across the room. She kicked off her shoes and wriggled out of her sweats while he reached for his belt. In less than a minute, they were naked on her bed, bodies straining to get closer than close.

"You love me, Cate," he said, taking her mouth again before she could affirm it. The rush, the long denial, the determination to claim sent them spiraling into the atmosphere almost before he entered her.

She cried out with pleasure and a second later, he released a groan that vibrated throughout her body. Cate held him tight, keeping him within her even after it was over.

"It'll never be over," Nick gasped. "Never."

He was right, Cate thought. She sensed his worry and his exhaustion. It had been a harrowing ten days for him.

"Not days." His voice husky, still breathless. "Months."

"Go to sleep, Nicky. I promise I'll be right here when you wake up."

To insure that, he withdrew, turned her back to him and locked his arms around her, one large, long-fingered hand resting on her breasts and the other curled around her thigh.

Cate smiled and snuggled back against him, anticipating the moment when he had enough rest to recover.

"Not long," he promised, lazily nipping her neck. "But the next session will be."

Cate cleared her mind and slept so that he would.

She woke to Nick's caresses, kept her eyes closed and simply enjoyed, lazily shifting into his touches as her arousal grew. They had never made love slowly, but he sure knew how. Fever pitch took on new meaning. Soon she was ready to beg.

He turned her gently and moved on top, sliding slowly into her while he braced above her on his arms. She watched his face, slipped into his mind and felt him probing hers. The connection was white light, minds and bodies in perfect union, pleasure so deep it pervaded every cell. Heaven, she thought. We're there.

He brought her to completion twice before he reached it, a slow, shuddering finale that did nothing to dispel the mood they'd created.

For a long time, he simply held her, his lips resting against her ear. No thoughts but languid fragments of newly formed memories, pleasure sliding into comfort.

They slept again and woke in each other's arms. Nick traced his tongue along the shell of her ear. "Your hair has grown," he whispered, and blew a strand of it off his lips. "I was afraid, if you were alive, that something else might grow." He palmed her abdomen and squeezed lightly. "We didn't use protection."

"I was on the pill," she said, stretching lazily. Female agents took precautions against the threat of rape if overpowered. And also against the possibility of an untimely pregnancy if they engaged in consensual sex. She didn't add any of that and hoped he hadn't been inside her head when she thought of it.

"Are you taking it now?" he asked quietly.

"No," she admitted. She raised onto her elbows and looked down at him.

Her priorities had changed so radically. Total independence wasn't all it was cracked up to be, it was just all she had known for so long. Now here was Nick, back in her life, offering her what no one else ever had or ever could. Loving her more than he loved himself. What more could a woman ask?

Nick had changed, too, or maybe she had never dug deep enough into his psyche to really know him when they were younger. She had never seen him face challenges the way he had in Italy. It was one thing to dive into the middle of a gunfight or shoot a terrorist to save somebody, if you were a trained agent and knew you wouldn't miss. But it took a helluva lot more courage to tackle that with no training at all. He was a doctor, not a fighter, but he made a damn good partner in any situation. What the hell was she waiting for?

"You want a life, Nicky? A real one with me? Maybe a couple of babies, a goofy old dog and occasional fights over who's gonna cook?"

He made a face. "You think I just showed up here to prove I was right? Of course I want a life with you. I'll stay here and open a practice in Boston." He paused. "Unless you're planning to go home and take your chances."

"No, I won't do that."

"Never?"

"Not ever. But I do have a plan. You know the very best place to hide when somebody's looking for you?"

"Where's that?"

Cate waved her fingers in a magician's flourish and grinned. "Somewhere they've already looked. Are you game?"

Nick kissed her soundly. "Baby, I'm game for anything."

Epilogue

Mercier dismissed the joint meeting of COMPASS and SEXTANT teams, but Vinland stayed behind, obviously wanting a word in private. "What is it, Eric?"

"Have you been keeping track of Nick Sandro? You know, Cate's doctor boyfriend?"

"Not for the past few months. I kept a watch for a while to make sure none of Adin's people were after him. Why?"

"I phoned his aunt—you know the one in Italy—to see if she knew how Nick was doing these days. Did you know he's gone to Colombia to volunteer medical services in a village down there?"

"He *what?*"

"Yeah." Eric sighed and shoved a hand through his hair until it came to rest on the back of his neck. "He took losing Cate really hard. Guess he couldn't take life as he knew it any longer. When I heard where he'd gone, I tried to connect with him, but no luck. Not so much as a whisper. You think we should send somebody down there after him, Jack? He won't last a month. Armed rebels, jungle rot, weird diseases and drugs all over the place. Joe has some real horror tales about that place."

Mercier slowly shook his head. "I can't risk an operative's life just because Sandro's trying to throw his away."

"You think this is a suicidal move?"

Mercier sighed and sat back, tapping his pen against his chin. "I think all Sandro ever wanted was to be with Cate. Since you can't make a mental connection, maybe he's already with her. Just let it go Eric. There's nothing we can do."

"I miss Catie," Eric said. "We all do. I sure wish she had flown back with us that day."

"Back to work," Jack ordered. "That's the best thing we can do in Cate's memory and I know for a fact that's what she'd want."

Meanwhile, a tall couple strolled hand in hand through an olive grove near a quaint red-roofed villa, reveling in the Tuscan sun and sharing plans for a brand-new life.

* * * * *

Here's a sneak peek at
THE CEO'S CHRISTMAS PROPOSITION,
the first in USA TODAY bestselling author
Merline Lovelace's HOLIDAYS ABROAD trilogy
coming in November 2008.

American Devon McShay is about to get the Christmas surprise of a lifetime when she meets her new client, sexy billionaire Caleb Logan, for the very first time.

Silhouette
Desire

Available November 2008

Her breath whistled out in a sigh of relief when he exited Customs. Devon recognized him right away from the newspaper and magazine articles her friend and partner Sabrina had looked up during her frantic prep work.

Caleb John Logan, Jr. Thirty-one. Six-two. With jet-black hair, laser-blue eyes and a linebacker's shoulders under his charcoal-gray cashmere overcoat. His jaw-dropping good looks didn't score him any points with Devon. She'd learned the hard way not to trust handsome heartbreakers like Cal Logan.

But he was a client. An important one. And she was willing to give someone who'd served a hitch in the marines before earning a B.S. from the University of

Oregon, an MBA from Stanford and his first million at the ripe old age of twenty-six the benefit of the doubt.

Right up until he spotted the hot-pink pashmina, that is.

Devon knew the flash of color was more visible than the sign she held up with his name on it. So she wasn't surprised when Logan picked her out of the crowd and cut in her direction. She'd just plastered on her best businesswoman smile when he whipped an arm around her waist. The next moment she was sprawled against his cashmere-covered chest.

"Hello, brown eyes."

Swooping down, he covered her mouth with his.

Sheer astonishment kept Devon rooted to the spot for a few seconds while her mind whirled chaotically. Her first thought was that her client had downed a few too many drinks during the long flight. Her second, that he'd mistaken the kind of escort and consulting services her company provided. Her third shoved everything else out of her head.

The man could kiss!

His mouth moved over hers with a skill that ignited sparks at a half dozen flash points throughout her body. Devon hadn't experienced that kind of spontaneous combustion in a while. A *long* while.

The sparks were still popping when she pushed off his chest, only now they fueled a flush of anger.

"Do you always greet women you don't know with a lip-lock, Mr. Logan?"

A smile crinkled the skin at the corners of his eyes. "As a matter of fact, I don't. That was from Don."

"Huh?"

"He said he owed you one from New Year's Eve two years ago and made me promise to deliver it."

She stared up at him in total incomprehension. Logan hooked a brow and attempted to prompt a nonexistent memory.

"He abandoned you at the Waldorf. Five minutes before midnight. To deliver twins."

"I don't have a clue who or what you're..."

Understanding burst like a water balloon.

"Wait a sec. Are you talking about Sabrina's old boy-friend? Your buddy, who's now an ob-gyn doc?"

It was Logan's turn to look startled. He recovered faster than Devon had, though. His smile widened into a rueful grin.

"I take it you're not Sabrina Russo."

"No, Mr. Logan, I am *not*."

* * * * *

Be sure to look for
THE CEO'S CHRISTMAS PROPOSITION
by Merline Lovelace.
Available in November 2008 wherever books are sold,
including most bookstores, supermarkets, drugstores
and discount stores.